DECISION OF THE HEART

DECISION OF THE HEART
•
ALMA BLAIR

AVALON BOOKS
THOMAS BOUREGY AND COMPANY, INC.
401 LAFAYETTE STREET
NEW YORK, NEW YORK 10003

© Copyright 1994 by Alma Blair
Library of Congress Catalog Card Number: 93-90922
ISBN 0-8034-9032-1
All rights reserved.
All the characters in this book are fictitious,
and any resemblance to actual persons,
living or dead, is purely coincidental.

PRINTED IN THE UNITED STATES OF AMERICA
ON ACID-FREE PAPER
BY HADDON CRAFTSMEN, SCRANTON, PENNSYLVANIA

To my sisters and lifelong friends,

Leona Penner and Darlene Moore

Chapter One

Erica Stone leaned her head back wearily against the plush seat of the small corporate jet as it whisked her ever nearer her destination of Willow Springs, Oklahoma. She was tired—physically and mentally. The past few weeks of intense negotiations were finally catching up with her. Slowly, with great effort, she closed her eyes and tried to relax.

But it was no use. The words of the maddening newspaper editorial she'd just read swam persistently through her mind. She opened her eyes and stared once more at the *Willow Springs Gazette* still open on her lap.

The piece had been written by the newspaper's editor, Jedidiah Daniels. The man had apparently taken it upon himself to fight the buyout her employer had planned—and ruin one of her own personal triumphs in the process.

Who would have thought she'd be pulled away from a multimillion-dollar merger in New York City and sent to act as troubleshooter in a godforsaken little place like Willow Springs? This was the most frustrating development so far in her rocketing career with Ledbetter Enterprises.

In fact, she was more than a little upset with B.J. Ledbetter, the firm's president, for ordering her away just as the merger was closing. She'd handled all the negotiations on the deal, and she longed to be there as her efforts came to fruition.

Still, B.J. was the boss—with a view of the big picture. Each merger, each buyout, each corporate takeover he engineered brought that big picture into sharper focus. So, if B.J. wanted some two-bit lawn mower company in Willow Springs, Oklahoma, there must be a sound reason for it. And Erica would do her best to see that the deal went through on schedule.

Public relations and mediation were her forte, and she had every confidence she'd be able to make this Jedidiah Daniels see reason—eventually.

Unfortunately, so far Daniels had shown no desire to be reasonable. Erica glanced down at the editorial again. It seemed he wasn't at all in favor of a big-city firm gobbling up a locally-owned business and moving control of that business out of state. He hinted that decisions made by management so far removed from the town might not be in the town's best interest. He totally ignored the fact that the business was floundering financially and badly needed an infusion of outside capital in order to compete in the current market.

Erica had spent the first part of the flight studying the prospectus on the buyout, and the deal appeared to be a rare and classic case where everyone involved would come out a winner. Too bad Daniels had chosen to step in and endanger the negotiations with his outmoded ideas.

But then, what else would one expect from a man called Jedidiah? The name sounded like it had been lifted straight out of a Victorian novel. It was just her luck to end up doing battle with an old dinosaur who refused to live in the twentieth century. He was probably at least eighty years old, wrinkled and deaf, and clinging to memories of the good old days.

Of course, he wouldn't have been able to interfere at all if the stock distribution of the company hadn't been set up as it was. Currently sixty percent of the stock was held by the plant's owner. The other forty percent had been bought up over the years by the employees through an Employee Stock Option Plan, or ESOP, as it was known in financial circles. Unfortunately, it took a three-fourths majority approval by the stockholders for the sale to go through—and the meeting to vote on the issue was only two weeks away.

At first all the employees had been in favor of the sale, but now opposition was growing, thanks mostly to Daniels. If he could rally enough support, the deal would fall through. B.J. would never settle for owning only a partial interest. And Erica didn't blame him. Trying to coordinate management decisions with so many stockholders would be a logistical nightmare.

Convincing such a group to sell might be just as big a nightmare—and it all fell on her. It was flattering that B.J. thought she could pull it off. That realization strengthened Erica's resolve to succeed. She would use every weapon at her disposal to do battle with Daniels the dinosaur.

She couldn't come on too strong, however. A man like Jedidiah Daniels would surely feel threatened by a take-charge female executive. Why, he probably still expected women to swoon at the mere mention of anything related to business.

Maybe this called for a different approach altogether. Impulsively she reached under the seat for her makeup case and opened the lid to study herself critically in the mirror. Jet-black hair was pulled severely away from a classic oval face, and large hazel eyes stared back levelly from behind hornrimmed glasses. The reflection was stark, crisp, businesslike—exactly the image she strove for in her New York office. At twenty-eight, she'd been forced to resort to such tricks to give herself credibility among her older, more experienced colleagues. But now some instinct told her the look was all wrong for Willow Springs, Oklahoma—and for Jedidiah Daniels.

If nothing else, she'd always had good instincts . . . and the courage to act upon them. That was one reason she'd risen so fast through the ranks to become B.J.'s top assistant. Though she wasn't a card player, she imagined her knack was akin to that possessed by a good poker player. In life, as in games of chance, winning didn't so much depend on being dealt a perfect hand as it did on playing the hand one was dealt *perfectly*.

After only a moment's deliberation, Erica reached up and unfastened the heavy gold clasp that held her hair back, allowing the thick black mane to fall in soft waves about her shoulders. She then loosened the navy print scarf knotted conservatively at her throat and opened the collar of her white silk blouse.

Normally she used very little makeup except for mascara and a touch of smoky gray eyeshadow. But that was too austere for this new look. She quickly added a soft coral blusher and matching lipstick.

Finally she removed the glasses and put them away in her purse. They were mostly for appearance anyway. The correction was so slight that she needed them only to avoid eyestrain when faced with extensive reading.

There. At last she was satisfied. And just in time. She felt the plane begin its descent in preparation for landing.

Decision of the Heart

As they dropped below the clouds, the gently rolling Oklahoma prairie took shape beneath them. A town Erica assumed to be Willow Springs materialized on the horizon and gradually grew larger. There was nothing remarkable about it. An orderly grid of residential streets branched out in all directions from a modest downtown business section. A patchwork of neatly plowed and planted farmland, dotted occasionally with clumps of trees, surrounded it.

With an unnerving jolt, she recognized that Willow Springs bore a superficial resemblance to her own hometown in upstate New York. Life in both places was probably equally slow-paced and boring. Again she was glad she'd managed to escape to the big city. She had no happy memories of her childhood or of life in a small town.

She quickly refocused on the present and noticed a busy four-lane interstate highway a few miles to the south of town. Easy access to the highway system had been mentioned as a plus in the prospectus. The metropolis of Oklahoma City lay roughly a hundred miles to the east—a scant two-hour drive. Considering that, perhaps the inhabitants of Willow Springs didn't feel quite as isolated as she'd felt growing up.

A tiny airport sat between the town and the highway. The pilot pointed the plane's nose unerringly down the one paved runway as they circled for a landing. Erica knew it would take all his skill to land safely on a runway intended only for small propeller-driven aircraft. But she never doubted he could do it. Though she didn't even know his name, she knew he was the best. B.J. Ledbetter employed nothing less. Which testified also to her own worth and competency. She shook off the insecurity she always felt when remembering her childhood and concentrated again on her mission.

As the plane settled smoothly to earth, she spotted her coworker, Allan Marshall, waiting at the edge of the runway. Allan was one of B.J.'s top accountants. Since negotiations with Lawn Magic Mowers began a few months ago, he'd made several trips to Willow Springs to verify assets and complete a perfunctory audit. On this latest excursion, he'd become aware of Daniels' assault on the sale and had alerted B.J. immediately. B.J. had then swiftly dispatched her to try to repair the damage.

Erica hoped Allan wouldn't object to her as B.J.'s choice. On occasion she still encountered men who resented her youth, gender, and status in the company hierarchy. There was also a chance that Allan might be jealous that she had use of the company jet. He'd always been forced to fly commercial airlines into Oklahoma City, then rent a car to complete the trip to Willow Springs. Of course, this was an emergency. Surely he'd understand.

She needn't have worried. Allan smiled a sincere welcome and hurried forward to help her with her luggage as she got off the plane. He was tall, thin, and attractive in a bookish way. He was fortyish and divorced—his wife's choice, not his. And though Erica didn't know him all that well, he seemed like a nice-enough guy.

He studied her now with a raised eyebrow as they hurried toward the only car in the small parking lot—a bright-red convertible. "This is a new look for you, isn't it, Erica? Softer. More feminine. It's a bit out of character, but I like it," he said thoughtfully.

Erica laughed, and patted the car. "Speaking of being out of character...."

Allan smiled sheepishly. "I know. But I wanted a convertible, and red's the only color they had at the car rental

Decision of the Heart

company. It's great driving around out here with the top down." He inhaled deeply. "Just breathe in that fresh air. No smog. No gasoline fumes. It's nothing like New York."

Erica laughed again. "I'll breathe later. Right now I have work to do."

"Gotcha." Allan threw her bags in the backseat and climbed in the car. "I got you an appointment with Daniels, like your secretary instructed when she called earlier to tell me you were on your way." He started the car. "The only trouble is, it's in fifteen minutes."

"Wow!" Erica exclaimed. "That's cutting it pretty close. What if the plane had been late?"

"I know, but it was the only time he had open." Allan pulled out of the parking area and headed toward town. "That paper of his is more or less a one-man operation. He's publisher, editor, reporter—you name it. You're lucky he agreed to see you at all on such short notice."

Of course, Erica thought, a man like Jedidiah Daniels would want to do everything himself. He wouldn't dare subscribe to such newfangled concepts as delegation of duty. He probably wouldn't trust an employee to do anything more important than mop the floor.

"Well, I suppose it's just as well to get this initial confrontation over as soon as possible," she mused out loud. "Are you staying?"

"Nope. I've taken my best shot at Daniels. He's all yours now."

"Thanks a lot."

Allan gave her a teasing wink. "Hey, you don't need me. Besides, I've got my hands full with Junior. He and I are in the middle of reviewing last year's accounts receivable. That guy's billing procedures are a joke."

"Junior?"

"Cecil Carver Jr., owner of Lawn Magic Mowers. His father, Cecil Carver Sr., founded the plant fifty years ago. Junior took over three years ago after the old man died."

"Three years ago is about when the profits started to decline, right?"

"Yep. Junior's not much of a businessman. He's more the genius inventor type. In fact, he designed most of the company's top products. He's just not good at the administrative end of running the plant. He knows it, too. That's why he wants out. Then with the money from the sale, he can hole up somewhere and invent weird contraptions to his heart's content."

"Yeah, *if* there is a sale," Erica muttered.

"That's where you come in." Allan continued his good-natured teasing. "I have every confidence you'll soon have Daniels eating out of your hand."

"I only hope that's true. Will you take my bags on over to the hotel before you head back to Junior?"

"No hotel. I'm staying at Hana's Boardinghouse, so I got you a room there, too—on a different floor, of course. These small-town people are big on appearances, and we have to maintain an air of propriety."

Erica made no comment. How well she remembered the small-town mentality. She glanced uneasily around at the quiet streets as they threaded their way toward the center of town. "There's not much to this place, is there?"

"Compared to New York, no. But it grows on you. The ambience kind of seeps in through your pores."

"Well, I think this fresh air and sunshine has affected your brain. Smog or no, it's the bright lights and big city for me," Erica said firmly.

"Yeah, me too, I guess. But I'm going to make the most of this while I'm here. You ought to, too. I've spent thousands of dollars on resort vacations and never felt as relaxed as I feel now."

Erica didn't reply. They'd entered the downtown area, and she knew her encounter with Jedidiah Daniels was at hand. A minute later Allan parked in front of an unpretentious red brick building located across the town square from an imposing old limestone courthouse. The sign over the awning read *Willow Springs Gazette*.

She quickly pulled down the visor mirror to check her appearance. She had a hairbrush in her purse, but decided against using it. Her wind-ruffled hair somehow added to the effect she was striving for.

She looked up to find Allan watching her. He chuckled. "Don't worry. You'll knock Daniels off his feet. The poor sucker won't know what hit him. That is what you intended, isn't it?"

So Allan was more perceptive than she'd first given him credit for being. It was Erica's turn to chuckle appreciatively as she followed him inside.

It was like stepping back in time. An old-fashioned oak counter separated the small lobby from the outer office. Behind the counter two older women worked at desks piled high with handwritten copy and proofs of typeset articles. Through a broad open door at the back of the building, Erica could see men operating a dated press which was noisily whirring off copies of the *Gazette*. There was no evidence of the sterile, computerized wizardry she'd glimpsed at other publishing efforts in New York City.

The women waved them through without comment when Allan announced the reason for their visit. He then led the way to an office off the pressroom. The lettering on the frosted glass pane in the door proclaimed *Editor*.

A commanding voice bellowed, "Come in," when Allan knocked. Erica squared her shoulders as Allan reached for the doorknob and gestured for her to precede him inside.

Once through the door, though, she stopped so short that Allan bumped into her. For her eyes locked with those of a man so virile and handsome her senses were reeling from the shock. His eyes were an unusual bright blue, and his hair was the color of the golden wheat fields she'd seen while driving into town. No doddering old-timer, this. He wasn't much past thirty. She felt totally unprepared to deal with this man.

Looking baffled, Allan gave her a nudge that set her moving on into the room. He then launched into introductions that eradicated all hope that there'd been some mistake. "Jedidiah Daniels, may I present my colleague, Erica Stone. Erica, this is Jed Daniels."

Jed offered his hand and said candidly, "I'll have to admit, Miss Stone, you're not at all what I expected."

Erica caught herself before she blurted a similar statement and managed a somewhat cool response. "And just what did you expect, Mr. Daniels?"

He continued to stare with open interest. "Oh, I don't know. . . . Perhaps glasses, a severe hairstyle, man-tailored suit. You know the type."

Erica laughed shakily and saw her discomfort hadn't escaped Allan. So Jed Daniels was sharp enough to come up with a much more accurate preconception of her than she'd had of him. That could mean she'd underestimated him in ways other than his physical appearance.

"It's refreshing," Jed continued, "to find a businesswoman who's not afraid to show her femininity."

Refreshing, perhaps, Erica thought. *But also dangerous.* She fought the urge to fumble in her purse for her glasses. She would've felt much safer behind them. However, it was too late to change tack. At least she'd been right in thinking this approach would throw him off guard. She just hadn't counted on putting herself at risk in the process. For it was almost impossible to concentrate with that flirtatious light there in Jed's eyes.

"Well, guess I'll be on my way." Allan's knowing grin made Erica want to strangle him. "Best wishes for a productive meeting. I'll see you later, Erica, and I'll see you tonight at the shindig, Jed."

Erica watched him go with growing panic. It took all her nerve to turn once again and face those incredible blue eyes. She lifted her briefcase in front of her as a barrier and pivoted slowly.

Jed was watching her curiously. "Well, Miss Stone, why don't you have a seat and tell me exactly what you wanted to see me about."

She sank stiffly into the chair he indicated. "Well, Mr. Daniels, my company is very concerned about your attack on our purchase of Lawn Magic Mowers. Mr. B.J. Ledbetter, the company president, hoped I might answer any questions you have about the transaction and put your fears to rest."

Jed leaned back in his chair with a wry smile. "I wouldn't exactly call my efforts an *attack*, Miss Stone. I'm merely trying to inject a note of caution. The main thing that bothers me is the rush. Why the big hurry to close the sale? Why not give the stockholders more time to consider it?"

"Well, to a man like Mr. Ledbetter, time is money. The funds he's placed in escrow could be earning greater interest elsewhere if the sale isn't going through. Besides, Mr. Ledbetter isn't the only one anxious to close. The company's owner is ready to get on with this, too," Erica said crisply.

"Ah, yes. Junior. He's not exactly the world's best businessman. He'd be the last one to know whether this is a sound move."

"So you've taken it upon yourself to protect him from his own stupidity, whether he wants your protection or not. Isn't that a bit pretentious?" she asked.

"I realize that to an outsider it must seem I'm meddling in things that don't concern me," he said condescendingly. "But I have to follow my conscience—particularly where the good of the town is concerned."

Erica was becoming very irritated by his high-handed manner. "It seems if you were truly concerned about the good of the town, you'd want new management at the plant. You said yourself that Mr. Carver is no businessman. The profits are declining each year. With my company in charge, all that could be reversed." She then launched into her well-rehearsed volley of statistics.

Jed interrupted her halfway through. "You're not telling me anything new, Miss Stone. I've read all your company's press releases about the sale. I even printed them in my newspaper, remember?"

"That was big of you," she replied caustically.

He seemed to be fighting a smile. "It *was* news, after all."

"Well, Mr. Daniels, if you know all the benefits Willow Springs could reap from the sale, why are you reluctant to endorse it?"

Decision of the Heart

"Call it a gut reaction. All this just seems too good to be true. I keep asking myself why a multimillion-dollar corporation is interested in our little plant. In other words, what's in it for your company, Miss Stone? Why is B.J. Ledbetter suddenly so obsessed with owning Lawn Magic Mowers?"

Try as she might, Erica couldn't keep the sarcasm out of her voice. "Actually, he didn't share that with me. Nor do I think it's important. It could be a pivotal part of his financial strategy for the year, or he could merely be buying it on a whim. He once bought a whole toy company because he wanted to give his grandson the same type of red wagon he'd played with as a child, and it was no longer being manufactured."

All humor was gone now from Jed's expression. "In other words, B.J. Ledbetter wants Lawn Magic Mowers, and it's your job to get him what he wants. No questions asked. It's nice you're able to be so blasé about a deal that, should it go awry, would wreck the economy of a whole town."

Erica realized she was letting this man get to her, and in so doing she was jeopardizing her mission. Mustering every shred of self-control she possessed, she managed to sound aloof and professional again as she continued.

"I didn't at all intend to sound blasé or uncaring, Mr. Daniels. I merely meant that I've worked with Mr. Ledbetter long enough to trust his judgment. Even moves which I've facetiously dubbed 'whims' have proven to be wise ones. For instance, the toy company I mentioned—the wagon he added to their line became one of their best-sellers. Profits from it were enough to put the company back on its feet. I can go on and on citing such examples if you'd care to listen. But the point I'm trying to make is that he's proven he can turn a failing company around. You should consider it fortunate he's interested in Willow Springs and stop trying to block a deal that can only be beneficial to everyone involved."

"I'm sorry, Miss Stone," Jed said stubbornly, "but I'm convinced we need to proceed with caution. You've heard the old saying, I'm sure—'Act in haste, repent in leisure'."

"And you've heard the old saying, I'm sure—'Don't look a gift horse in the mouth'," she shot back.

"Touché." Humor danced momentarily in his eyes before he grew serious. "However, you can't deny your company sees Lawn Magic Mowers abstractly as figures on a profit and loss statement. They have no emotional investment whatsoever in the town or the people."

"I'll admit that's true to some extent, but that might be beneficial in the long run. This local intimacy you talk about may be part of the problem. You, the townspeople, and especially the present plant management might be too emotionally involved. An outsider's objectivity might prove very advantageous in making the decisions necessary if the company is to survive."

"*If* the company is to survive, Miss Stone? You see, it's that 'if' that concerns me. There should be no if about it. Lawn Magic Mowers *must* survive, or Willow Springs will become a ghost town. That's why I think we should keep control of the plant here locally where the people in charge will have a vested interest in seeing that it does indeed continue in operation."

"Well, Mr. Daniels, perhaps it's good that decision isn't yours to make. Luckily the stockholders will decide. And I plan to see that they hear both sides—not just the slanted rhetoric you've been printing in your editorials."

"That plan might be hard to implement from a plush office in New York."

"Indeed it might. That's why I've come to stay for a while."

To her complete bafflement, he actually seemed pleased. "What?" he chided with a teasing smile. "Aren't you afraid of losing your famed outsider's objectivity if you spend any time here?"

Erica longed to make some snide remark in response, but she refused to be goaded into something she'd regret later. "I'm glad you find this so humorous, Mr. Daniels. And while you're in such a good mood, I have a proposition for you. You intimated earlier that you were a newsman above all else, and thus felt obligated to print stories with which you personally disagreed. Well, how about taking that professed fairness one step further. Let me buy space on tomorrow's editorial page to respond to the points you've made so far against the sale of the plant. Sort of a debate in print."

Jed shrugged. "Far be it from me to turn down advertising dollars. But don't fool yourself into thinking that will be enough. The printed opinions of a stranger won't carry much weight with the townspeople."

"Well, perhaps I won't be such a stranger by the time the vote is taken."

"My, my. You're staying two whole weeks. You *are* committing to an all-out effort." The amusement then faded from his eyes to be replaced by something smoldering and provocative. "I guess this means the battle lines are drawn."

Erica's heart skipped a beat. It was all she could do to continue to meet his sorcerous gaze. But she was determined not to let him see the effect he was having on her. "Yes, I suppose it does."

"Then shall we make the first skirmish tonight at the town picnic—the 'shindig' Allan mentioned as he was leaving? The whole town usually turns out for it, and the question of the sale will invariably come up. I intend to be there circulating, giving my views on the matter."

She felt triumphant as she managed to respond without even blinking. "It's a date, Mr. Daniels. I can circulate with the best of them."

So the challenge had been issued and accepted—on far more levels than Erica cared to consider.

Perhaps her earlier analogy when she'd classed Jed as a dinosaur hadn't been too wrong. For as she sat across from him now, he looked to her like a very dangerous creature indeed. A tyrannosaurus, perhaps. And she'd come poorly prepared to do battle with him. True, the sword of her business prowess was honed to perfection. But the shield guarding her emotions was already badly dented by the piercing onslaught of physical and emotional attraction that sizzled between her and Jed. She'd barely managed to hold her own in this initial confrontation, and the real combat had not yet begun.

That did not bode at all well for the outcome of the war.

Chapter Two

Erica felt a flood of relief as she stepped out onto the sun-scorched sidewalk from the *Gazette* building. She'd managed to escape with her dignity intact, which was a minor miracle considering how unprepared she'd been for Jed Daniels.

She glanced around for a taxi stand, but none was in sight. She felt a new surge of irritation. She wanted to put some distance between herself and the provocative Mr. Daniels—fast.

But that wasn't to be. She heard the door open behind her, and could tell by the uncanny prickle running up her spine that it was Jed. She fought the urge to flee in a giggling adolescent panic. Instead she forced a smile and turned to face him.

"Is Allan picking you up?" he asked.

"No, he's busy at the factory. I'll just take a taxi."

Jed again seemed amused. "Willow Springs is a small town, Miss Stone. It doesn't have a taxi service."

"Then I'll walk," she said tightly. "How far is Hana's Boardinghouse?"

"It's about six blocks that way." He pointed vaguely, then indicated an aging station wagon parked at the curb. "Come on. I'll give you a lift."

She remembered Allan's statement about Jed's tight

schedule. "I really can't impose like that, Mr. Daniels. Besides, I enjoy walking."

The teasing twinkle in Jed's eyes intensified. "In those shoes?"

Erica had to admit her expensive high heels were hardly made for a six-block trek. But the last thing her frazzled nerves needed was another stint alone with this maddeningly attractive man.

"What's the matter?" he prodded. "Afraid of being accused of consorting with the enemy?" His smile broadened as she glared at him. "Sorry. I couldn't resist. And I assure you, you won't be imposing at all."

Erica hated the idea of being indebted to him, but he was right. She had no other choice. Reluctantly she stalked over to the car and got in.

Jed glanced over at her as he pulled away from the curb. "I realize I shouldn't be giving you such a hard time, but you leave yourself wide open for it. Did anyone ever tell you that you take things far too seriously?"

The sarcasm crept back into her voice. "But didn't we just establish in your office that this is serious business, Mr. Daniels? The economy of a whole town at stake, et cetera, et cetera. . . . "

"Ouch!" He chuckled. "You sure know how to make a guy eat his words." His tone changed subtly. "I guess I was just hoping that we could separate business from pleasure and still be friends."

She glowered at him again. Surely he didn't really think that was possible. The smile he flashed her testified that he did—and sent a flutter all the way to the pit of her stomach.

Thankfully the ride was a short one. Jed pulled to a stop in front of a quaint old Victorian mansion, and Erica's agitation lessened at the sight of it. She collected Victorian antiques, and her interest quite naturally extended to houses of the same era. Staying here might be the one bright spot of the trip.

"I'll go in with you and introduce you to Hana Giles, the owner," Jed announced cheerfully. "She'll have you revived and refreshed in plenty of time for the picnic. I could even pick you up if you like."

His offer took Erica by surprise. Was he asking her for a date? If so, he was certainly waging this war in a peculiar manner. Even more peculiar, she found the thought of going out with him strangely appealing. However, it certainly wouldn't be prudent under the circumstances. "I don't think that would be a good idea," she hedged as she got out of the car.

He shrugged. "Okay, suit yourself."

As they walked up the sidewalk, a plump, matronly woman opened the door in greeting. "Hi, Hana," Jed called. "I'm just delivering your new boarder. This is Erica Stone."

Hana smiled warmly. "Welcome, Miss Stone. I've been watching for you since Allan dropped your bags off. I've got you all settled in upstairs."

Jed winked at Erica. "See? You're in good hands. Guess I'd better be off to cover my story."

"You headed over to talk to Will Harris about those tires that got stolen out of his garage last night?" Hana asked.

Jed fixed her with a mock glower. "How'd you know about that?"

Hana chuckled. "Heard the news at Emma's beauty shop this morning."

"I'll swear," Jed growled comically, "this town doesn't

need a newspaper as long as we have Emma as unofficial town cryer."

"And ain't she good at it, too?" Hana teased. "Been meaning to ask you, Jed, how's Sadie and the little ones?"

Erica had been only half listening to this point, but now her interest picked up considerably. Sadie? Little ones? Why, it had never occurred to her that Jed might be married.

He grinned. "They're all fine. Growing like weeds, naturally."

"Guess I kinda lost track. How many did you end up with?" Hana asked.

"Four. And don't remind me."

Four children! Erica tried not to react. Apparently Jed didn't believe in population control. Another sign of his dated thinking.

Hana laughed. "Now, you know you're crazy about the whole bunch."

"That I am," Jed admitted. "Well, I'll see you ladies tonight. Let me know, Erica, if you change your mind and want me to pick you up."

Erica looked up sharply at his switch to her first name. The unsettling spark of challenge was back in his eyes. She met it icily. He had some nerve thinking she'd become involved with a married man. "Thank you, *Mr.* Daniels. But I can't make any definite plans until I check with Allan."

His smile broadened bewitchingly, and Erica's heart gave an unsettling lurch in response. "Hey, I was just trying to be neighborly," he said as he sauntered off down the sidewalk.

Erica bristled at his arrogance. The unmitigated gall of the man!

Hana led the way inside. "Land sakes, Miss Stone, you coulda knocked me over with a feather when you came driving up here with Jed. I expected you two to start sparring the minute you met—since you're on opposite sides of the fence and all."

"So you know why I'm here?" Erica asked in surprise.

"Sure. The whole town knows. Well, your room's right this way."

Erica glimpsed an old-fashioned parlor to the left and a big, sunny dining room to the right as she followed Hana down the hallway. Both rooms were furnished with authentic period pieces—all of which, Erica knew, would have brought a nice price at the antique stores she frequented in New York. She longed to ask Hana about them, but didn't want to divert the conversation from the present topic. Hana's ramblings were bound to give her a better feel for what she was up against.

"Yep," Hana continued as she huffed her way up the gleaming mahogany staircase to the second floor, "when Jed started them editorials, we all knew your company would send someone to try to mend fences. Junior let the word out it was to be a woman. We just didn't expect anyone so young and pretty."

Erica tensed in spite of Hana's flattering words and friendly tone. So the reasons for her trip were common knowledge. She should have expected as much. How well she remembered the small town propensity for gossip. But in this instance, maybe it wasn't all that bad. At least it meant there was a high level of interest in the sale.

Hana paused at the top of the stairs to catch her breath. "You were pretty smart to start right off trying to get on

Jed's good side. Guess you done figured out that if you win him over, the rest of the town will follow."

Erica decided Hana was pretty smart herself to have guessed her reason for contacting Jed. Of course, she didn't volunteer that she'd soon abandoned that scheme as too dangerous and had subsequently done her best to brush Jed off. She only laughed hollowly. "You guessed my plan, all right."

"I thought so!" Hana chortled. "And it was the best move you could've made. People hereabouts trust Jed. You convince *him* you're on the up-and-up, and the battle's nearly won."

Erica suddenly felt a sinking sensation in the pit of her stomach. Apparently there was no getting around the fact that Jed's opposition was the main obstacle to the sale. But perhaps there was a way to win the town over without him. And if she pumped Hana, she might find it. She donned her most earnest expression. "How do you feel personally about the sale, Hana?"

The woman grew thoughtful as she shuffled off down the hallway. "I'm sorta undecided. Like most folks in town, I own a little stock myself. My husband worked for the plant before he died, and I inherited his shares. I wouldn't at all be against selling and making a tidy profit. But I don't guess I'd do it if I thought I'd be harming the town. And I'll have to admit, Jed's editorials have made me stop and think. The rest of the town feels pretty much the same way."

Erica's stomach gave a final queasy lurch. Darn that Jed Daniels! How had he become so influential in the first place? "I suppose Mr. Daniels has lived here all his life," she probed subtly.

"Nope. He only moved to town a few years ago to take

Decision of the Heart

over the paper after his grandfather died. Turned the old *Gazette* around, he did. Helped the rest of us do the same with our businesses. It was his idea for me to start advertising in them bed-and-breakfast guidebooks and put up some billboards out along the interstate highway. Well, it worked. Lures the tourists in pretty regular now. And once they taste my home cooking, they're hooked—they stop by on their next trip through. Jed's got a heap of business savvy, I'll give him that." Hana stopped at the end of the hall and threw open the door. "Well, this is it. Best in the house. Hope you like it."

Erica did indeed like it. A high mahogany bed, ornately carved, stood in one corner. A matching nightstand, wardrobe, and dresser completed the furnishings. The room reminded her of her own bedroom at home. Yes, this was much preferable to the cold, impersonal hotels where she usually stayed on business trips. She smiled at Hana. "It's absolutely beautiful."

Hana beamed. "Thanks. I had my helper, Mary, unpack for you. She's a good worker—usually does a nice job on stuff like that. You'll be sharing a bath with the room next door. The room's unoccupied at the moment. But when you're in the bathroom, you ought to get in the habit of locking the connecting door just to ensure your privacy."

"Yes, I'll do that. By the way, do you know when Allan will be back?"

"Well, he usually stays pretty late at the factory, but tonight I know he plans on attending our town picnic." A sly smile spread across the woman's face. "From Jed's parting remarks, I gather you do, too. Smart move. It'll be a good way to meet lots of people fast." She eyed Erica's designer suit. "You'll need to wear something more casual, though—jeans or shorts maybe."

"I didn't bring either. I thought this trip was strictly business."

"Honey, getting in good with the townspeople better be your first order of business. You're about the same size as my daughter. She's away at college now, but she left a bunch of her clothes here. I'll have Mary bring up some things for you to wear."

"Thanks. That's very kind." Erica smiled. "I'll see you at the picnic."

"That's the spirit. I'm going over now to help set up. It starts at six. Don't be late."

"I'll try not to be. I guess it all depends on Allan, though."

Hana chuckled. "Well, if he's late, you can always call Jed for a lift."

Yes, wouldn't his wife like that, Erica thought. She said only, "I'll phone Allan in a few minutes and ask about his plans."

"Yeah, that might be best. There's a pay phone in the downstairs hall, and the plant's phone number is in the book."

Erica stepped out of her uncomfortable high heels as Hana pulled the door shut behind her. She placed her briefcase on the dresser and extracted a legal pad. She needed to work on her editorial for tomorrow's paper. She only hoped she wasn't too tired to think clearly. This could be as important as any corporate report she'd ever prepared. Her fleecy robe was hanging neatly in the wardrobe among her other clothes. Mary had done a good job unpacking. She quickly changed and turned back the bedspread. She arranged the pillows into a fluffy backrest and snuggled into the cushy nest with a contented sigh. Heavenly! She yawned in spite of herself.

Maybe this wasn't such a good place to work after all. But she couldn't force herself to get up. Nor could she fight off the drowsiness that rolled in like a gray fog to blur the blank page before her. Oh, well, she could take a quick nap and still get the editorial written before the picnic. She laid the pad aside and pulled the sheet up over her.

As she drifted off to sleep, Jed Daniels' face floated into her mind and lingered there. A delicious tingle warmed her as she wondered how it would feel to be held in his arms. And she couldn't summon the willpower to dismiss the image from her mind. It was simply too pleasurable.

However, as sleep deepened, the pleasurable sensation fast deteriorated into something not so delightful. She and Jed were being pursued through a crowd of snickering townspeople by an angry, faceless Sadie Daniels and four tearful, blond children—all the image of Jed, of course. Erica kept trying to glimpse Sadie's face, but Jed was dragging her along so fast she couldn't get a good look. And he wouldn't let go of her, no matter how loudly she protested. They just kept running and running....

Her heart was pounding unpleasantly by the time she was awakened by a persistent knocking at the door. "Who is it?" she called, struggling to become more fully awake.

"It's Mary. Mrs. Giles asked me to bring you a change of clothes."

As Erica stumbled groggily across the room, she noticed she'd been asleep for almost two hours. When she opened the door, she saw a girl of around fifteen, with a pretty face, huge brown eyes, and a shy, vulnerable look about her. Mary thrust the clothes at Erica without comment and turned to go. The abrupt action took Erica by surprise, but she recovered enough to call after her, "Mary, you did a nice job unpacking my things."

The briefest of smiles lit the girl's face. "Thanks."

Erica then thought to ask about Allan. "Do you know if Mr. Marshall has come back yet?"

"No, ma'am, he hasn't," Mary replied, then hurried off down the stairs.

"Great," Erica muttered as she shut the door. "I hope he's back by the time I get ready." She checked her watch again. Almost five o'clock. She'd have to wait to write her editorial. In fact, she barely had time to make the picnic by six. She hurried into the adjoining bathroom to run the tub full of steaming water.

Her enthusiasm for attending the picnic had diminished even further since her nap. The disturbing dream had left her listless and depressed. It didn't take much intelligence to discern the symbolism of it all, she admitted ruefully as she sank into the tub. Clearly it pictured her fear that her feelings for Jed might drag her places she didn't want to go. If that happened, innocent people like Jed's wife and children would be angered and hurt.

And worse, she'd be the laughingstock of the whole town. Perhaps that was the thing she feared most. She'd learned growing up that there were no secrets in a small town. Everyone knew everything about everybody.

She gave an involutary shudder—then promptly reprimanded herself.

Nothing like that was going to happen. Although she was overwhelmingly attracted to Jed, she had no intention of acting on that attraction. Her own strict moral code aside, an affair with a married man was a one-way street to disaster.

And she'd been ridiculed enough as a child to know better than to ever again deliberately put herself in a situation that invited such ridicule and gossip.

But even as she settled the issue mentally, she acknowledged that it might not be so easy to accomplish. Over the next two weeks, she needed to get close enough to Jed to influence him, but not so close that she'd be caught in the deadly undertow of emotion that swirled between them. It would be like walking a tightrope. But she vowed she would manage to do it somehow.

Determinedly she got out of the tub, noticing too late that she'd forgotten to lock the door to the adjoining bedroom. Oh, well, since it was unoccupied it didn't matter. She scrubbed herself dry and donned the clothes Hana had sent. The Western jeans, white cotton shirt, and red sneakers all fit perfectly. It had been years since she'd had on a pair of jeans. But as she eyed herself appraisingly in the mirror, she had to admit they showed off her figure as none of her expensive tailored slacks ever could.

She tied a red silk scarf around her neck bandanna style and was ready to go. Hopefully, Allan was, too. She was on her way down the stairs to search out his room when he burst through the front door.

He whistled his approval of her outfit. "Wow! You're just full of surprises on this trip, Erica. I gather from that getup that you *are* going to the picnic. I intended to bang on your door as soon as I got ready and invite you, but I didn't much expect you to accept."

"Why not, for heaven's sake?"

"Well, honestly, you don't quite seem the type who'd go for a town picnic in the park. You're more the champagne supper at the Ritz type."

Erica smiled benignly. If he only knew her background. ... But he didn't. And she planned to keep it that way. "Well, when in Rome, do as the Romans do—especially when you need the Romans' approval for a vital project. So slip into your jeans and let's be on our way."

He looked at his watch. "Golly, I *am* running late. Sorry about that. I got sidetracked trying to determine how much Junior should get for the patents he has pending. He really needs to ask more money for them."

"More money!" Erica cried. "Hey, whose side are you on, anyway?"

Allan laughed. "I know it's crazy. But the guy's such a babe in the woods, he brings out my fatherly instincts, I guess. You'll see what I mean when you meet him. He'll be at the picnic tonight, by the way."

Erica cleared her throat. "Speaking of the picnic. . . . "

Allan grimaced. "You know, it's going to take me half an hour to get ready. Why don't you take the car and go on ahead. The park's right at the end of this street. You can't miss it. I'll just walk over."

"But I was counting on you to make introductions," Erica protested.

"I wouldn't be much help there, anyway. I've spent most of my time at the factory, and I haven't met many people. Just latch onto Hana—or better yet, Jed. He'll be glad to introduce you around. I'll be there shortly."

"Great!" Erica muttered as he charged off down the hall. Didn't anyone besides herself recognize the irony of asking the man who created the problem to help her solve it? And what about that fabled, small-town sense of propriety? Hana and Allan both were practically throwing her at a married man.

Decision of the Heart

She left the house determined to get her tumultuous feelings under control. Surely she was overreacting, reading more into everyone's actions than she should. Hana, Allan, and even Jed might be acting innocently.

Maybe her attraction to Jed was all one-sided—but so intense that it was causing her to misinterpret the things he did and said. Maybe he hadn't been flirting with her at all. Maybe he *was* just being neighborly in offering to take her to the picnic. If she'd accepted, he might well have pulled up in a car loaded with his wife and kids.

Which really would have been hard to deal with.

Oh, this situation was hopeless! With a feeling of impending doom, she started the car and pulled away from the curb. One thing was for certain. This picnic was definitely not going to be any picnic for her.

Chapter Three

The uneasy feeling intensified when Erica arrived at the park. An intimidating throng was milling about under the ancient elm trees. Children were cavorting on the playground equipment; teenagers had a baseball game going in one corner of the grounds; a group of old men had gathered around a horseshoe pit where a match was in progress. It would be no easy task locating Hana in a crowd this size. Already Erica regretted coming alone. She should have just waited for Allan.

"You look like a young lady in need of an escort," a hauntingly familiar voice rumbled beside her. "Will I do?"

She turned slowly to confront Jed Daniels. "Fancy bumping into you right off the bat. What a coincidence."

"No coincidence. I've been watching for your car. Thought you'd feel like a lost sheep wandering around in such a crowd."

"Your selfless concern for my welfare is very touching."

He ignored her sarcasm. "Oh, I wasn't thinking of you alone. I had a selfish motive. I wanted to latch onto you before some other guy did."

Erica's sense of foreboding increased. She'd been right all along. He was definitely flirting with her. She battled the urge to remind him he was a married man. Tempting as it was, she couldn't risk offending him.

She decided to try to be tactful. "Won't people think it strange that you're 'consorting with the enemy,' as you so cleverly put it earlier?"

"Not when they see how beautiful the enemy is. They'd probably think me crazy if I didn't consort just a little." He winked roguishly. "Well, Miss Stone, are you ready to meet the good people of Willow Springs?"

He was forcing her to be blunt. "Actually, I'd rather Hana showed me around. If you'll point her out to me—"

"I'm afraid Hana's in charge of the food tables, and she takes that duty very seriously. I doubt you'll be able to pry her away. So, I guess you're stuck with me."

"So it would appear." She sighed in resignation. "Well, lead on."

"I hardly expected you to yield yourself so readily into my clutches."

She glowered at him.

Jed cleared his throat. "Right. I keep forgetting this is serious business. Why don't we start by introducing you to the mayor?"

He took her arm and marched her briskly toward a cluster of middle-aged couples a short distance away. A distracting tingle surged through Erica's body from his hand on her elbow. She longed to jerk away from him, but knew she couldn't without making a scene. The group turned expectantly as they charged up. Without preamble, Jed began introductions. To her dismay, Erica realized the names were flying past her without registering. What had happened to her concentration?

She cut her eyes at Jed. It was a silly question.

Summoning her nerve, she shrugged out of his grip in time to hear the names of the mayor and his wife—Frank and Vivian Ferris. She felt strangely triumphant and in charge again. She glanced at Jed and found the teasing twinkle back in his eyes. The man was so infuriating! But she couldn't allow him to distract her. Mayor Ferris and friends were eyeing her curiously and not unkindly, which was promising.

The mayor, a distinguished-looking older man, spoke up first. "Well, Miss Stone, we were hoping your company would send someone to address the serious questions our *young* newspaper editor here has raised. Even though I'm not a stockholder, I'd like to go on record in support of the sale." He threw Jed a hostile look. "I believe new management would improve production at the plant, and that in turn would help the economy of the whole town."

Erica was quick to realize the mayor's reaction might indicate that at least a portion of the population was on her side. Perhaps she'd been premature in her appraisal of Jed's support in the community. She sprang into action. "Actually, Mayor, though we at Ledbetter Enterprises appreciate Mr. Daniels' concern, we want to reassure all of you that the fears he's expressed about our commitment to the town are unfounded."

"That so?" The mayor sent another disparaging look Jed's way.

"Most assuredly. If we buy the plant, we're in for the long haul." Erica was pleased to see the knot of people around them growing. This was exactly the forum she needed to win support for her cause. She raised her voice and launched into her canned list of expected benefits to the town—the one Jed had refused to listen to at his office. She kept a wary eye on him, halfway expecting him to interrupt. However, he didn't seem at all bothered that she'd gained an impromptu audience. But again she'd barely gotten started when the clanging of the dinner bell caused the crowd to stir restlessly and cast longing glances at the food tables.

She had no choice but to stop. "Thank you for your attention," she finished lamely. "Perhaps I'll have the opportunity to continue later."

"Well, we'll just see that you do," the mayor spoke up. "In fact, this issue is of sufficient importance that we might arrange for you to address an open town meeting. You'd all come, right, folks?"

There was a murmur of assent—not nearly the enthusiastic response Erica had hoped for, but it was a start.

"I think we ought to let Jed Daniels speak at the same meeting," an anonymous voice called from the back of the crowd. This time the murmur of response sounded unanimous. "You game for a debate, Jed?" the voice asked.

"Sure thing." Jed seemed more than pleased by the suggestion. "And surely there are other clubs that would want to hear from Miss Stone and myself. You'd be agreeable, wouldn't you, Miss Stone?" The same arrogant challenge was back in his eyes.

"Of course." Erica tried to match his tone of voice exactly. He was up to something, but she couldn't imagine what. Surely he knew he was playing right into her hands by arranging these speaking engagements. Unless he thought she couldn't measure up to him as a public speaker. In which case, he had another think coming.

"You could speak to the Kiwanis Club," someone called from the crowd.

"And the Ladies Auxiliary," yelled another. "And the Rotary Club...."

"Sounds like you folks plan to keep these two pretty

busy," the mayor interrupted. "I'm sure they'd like to hear from all of you. Now, let's hit the food line and get down to some serious eating."

As the people dispersed, Erica saw Allan standing a few feet away. She hurried to join him while Jed lingered with his supporters.

Allan smiled as she walked up. "No wonder B.J. likes you to handle these situations, Erica. You have an earnest credibility about you."

"Thanks . . . I think." Erica thought she'd detected a hint of cynicism in his voice, but she didn't have time to question it. The eerie, prickly sensation racing up her spine signalled that Jed was moving in on her again. She pulled Allan toward the food tables. "You must be starved. Let's go eat."

Allan glanced over his shoulder. "Hey, looks like Jed's trying to catch up to us. Want to wait for him?"

"No!" she cried, causing Allan to raise a questioning eyebrow. But he tactfully said nothing, for which she was grateful. They managed to go through the serving line before Jed could overtake them. Erica watched distractedly as Hana and associates piled her plate high with fried chicken, baked beans, coleslaw, and rolls. She then headed unerringly toward a crowded table with only two empty seats left. Allan followed along without comment. Out of the corner of her eye, she watched Jed take a seat a few tables away. Perhaps he'd gotten her not-so-subtle hint.

Predictably, the others at the table seemed awed that the "big-city folks" had chosen them as dinner companions. They voiced a polite but restrained welcome, then excused themselves as soon as they'd finished eating. Soon Erica and Allan were left sitting alone. A wary glance at Jed revealed he was now caught up in conversation at his table, so Erica was able to relax a little.

"Best food I've ever tasted," Allan proclaimed with a satisfied sigh.

Erica mumbled her agreement. Surprisingly, she'd eaten everything on her plate, but couldn't recall how it had tasted. She simply had to get a grip on herself. Starting now! She gave Allan her undivided attention.

"Look at them." A sadness crept into his voice as he studied the crowd. "All the secure little family units. Since I've been here, I've wondered if things might've worked out differently for Peg and me in a town like this."

"This place isn't utopia, you know," Erica exclaimed. "The divorce rate is probably as high here as it is in New York."

"I seriously doubt it." Allan's gaze settled on a young couple pushing a giggling little boy in a swing. "The lifestyle here is so different. Here traditional family values are still something to be treasured."

"Don't be too sure," Erica scoffed. "I'll bet Willow Springs has its share of two-timing spouses just like the big cities do." She cut her eyes at Jed. "Besides, Allan, if you and Peg were incompatible in New York, you'd be incompatible here, too."

He sighed. "I suppose. But incompatibility wasn't really the cause of our divorce. I was gone from home so much with this job that we never had a chance to see whether we were compatible or not."

His agonizing was cut short as a frantic voice called to him out of the gathering dusk. "Allan! Thank heavens I've finally found you!"

Erica saw a thin, balding little man with thick glasses

hurrying toward them. His rumpled business suit looked strangely out of place amid the casually dressed crowd. But she suspected he would've looked out of place in any setting, no matter how he was dressed. She smiled at Allan. "Junior?"

He nodded. "Junior." He rose as the little man puffed to a stop. "I wondered what was keeping you, Junior. I'd like you to meet Erica Stone."

"How do you do, Miss Stone," Junior mumbled distractedly before continuing. "Oh, Allan, it's a disaster! A whole month's sales receipts have disappeared from the files. I'm afraid I completely lost my temper with Mrs. Patterson over the matter, and she quit!"

"Now, calm down, Junior," Allan soothed. "Mrs. Patterson's leaving might be a blessing. She had to be the world's worst secretary."

"But Father had every confidence in her."

Allan winked at Erica across Junior's shoulder. "Well, that was probably back when she could still see and hear. How old is she anyway—ninety?"

"Oh, no. Not nearly that old. Eighty, maybe...."

Allan was trying desperately not to laugh. "So, see? She was long past retirement. Don't worry. We'll find someone to replace her, and we'll find the missing file, too."

"Can we look for it now? Things just seem to be getting more and more out of hand. It's only two weeks until your Mr. Ledbetter wants all the paperwork completed on the sale. Another of those nasty reminders from him came over the fax machine as I was leaving the plant."

Allan's shoulders slumped in resignation. "Yeah, I guess we'd better check into it tonight." He turned to Erica. "I'll

Decision of the Heart

leave you the car and ride with Junior. He can drop me off when we're done. Enjoy the picnic."

"Thanks, but I doubt if I'll stay much longer. I'm still pretty tired." She looked pointedly at Junior. "Good luck."

"Yeah. See you." Allan draped an arm around Junior's shoulders as they walked away. "You had anything to eat yet, Junior? Then let's stop by the food tables and get Hana to fix you a plate to take with us. . . . "

Erica recalled Allan's earlier comment about Junior bringing out his fatherly instincts. True enough, she thought, as the unlikely duo disappeared into the crowd.

"They make quite a pair," Jed's voice rumbled from behind her. She looked up in surprise as he slid nonchalantly onto the bench beside her.

"Yes, they do," she replied stiffly. She'd let him get much too close again. She should have left with Allan. Now there was no graceful way to escape. "Well, if you'll excuse me," she said awkwardly, preparing to rise.

He laid a restraining hand on her arm. "Miss Stone, are you trying to avoid me?"

"Of course not," she lied.

The flirtatious gleam was back in his eyes. "Then stay for a while. There'll be live music later. I'll teach you to square dance."

His hand seemed to be searing into her flesh. Her frazzled nerves were stretched to the breaking point, and she was tired of being civil to this insensitive womanizer! She pulled away and stood up. "I have no desire to learn to square dance. Now, I really must go."

He rose and caught her arm again. "Hey, what's wrong with you, anyway?"

She stared at him in disbelief. He certainly had the look

of injured innocence down pat. "There's nothing wrong with me, Mr. Daniels. But there's something very wrong with you if you think I'm stupid enough to get involved with a married man." His look of innocence changed to one of confusion. No doubt he was wondering how she'd found out. "Remember, I heard you and Hana discussing your wife, Sadie, and your youngsters?"

He eyes narrowed shrewdly, and a spark of something she couldn't quite identify flared into them. Perhaps it was respect for her. He probably hadn't expected her to call his bluff. "So you know about Sadie," he said with infuriating calm. "Well, then let's get this whole matter out in the open. I live right across the street, there in that house on the corner. Let's go over now, and you can meet Sadie."

"I-I don't think that's a good idea—" Erica blustered.

"Oh, I insist." His grip tightened on her arm, and once again she saw no dignified way of escaping. As he steered her toward the small white clapboard house, she had the eerie sensation of reliving her dream. Here she was being dragged along by Jed Daniels into an embarrassing situation. Oh, well, one thing for certain. After this, if Sadie Daniels appeared in her nightmares, the woman would at least have a face.

As Jed opened the front door, Erica noticed absently that it wasn't locked. She thought about the string of deadbolts on her apartment door in New York. Allan was right—there were some marked differences in the life-style here.

Jed motioned her into the clean but sparsely furnished living room, then called down the hall. "Sadie, Sadie! I'm back." There was a flurry of activity in the hallway, and a furry black-and-white mongrel hurtled around the corner

Decision of the Heart 39

and flung herself into Jed's arms. "This, Miss Stone, is Sadie," he said from behind the fur.

Erica knew her mouth was gaping open, yet she felt absolutely powerless to close it. "Why, it's a dog!" she sputtered.

A self-satisfied grin settled over Jed's face. "I would've told you sooner, but you acted so self-righteous over there in the park. I just had to see the look on your face when you found out."

Erica bristled. "You seem to be enjoying quite a bit of amusement today at my expense, Mr. Daniels. And since I don't particularly enjoy being laughed at, I think I'll go."

"Erica, wait—" He put the dog on the floor and took Erica by the shoulders. "I'm sorry. I realize you don't yet know how to react to my sense of humor. But you'll get used to it . . . in time."

Despite everything, she felt a tingle of excitement at the subtle promise of his words. But she was entering dangerous territory again. She had to keep him at a distance if she wanted to preserve her sanity. She shrugged away from him. "I really need to be going."

He pointed at Sadie. "Don't you want to see the 'youngsters'?"

Erica stared down at the appealing little creature and decided to risk a glimpse at the pups. "Oh, I suppose. Then my humiliation will be complete."

Sadie danced along in the lead as they headed down the hall. Erica noticed that the rooms they passed were pleasant, but equally as bare as the living room. Jed glanced back and caught her in a curious stare.

"Wondering about my lack of household goods?" he asked affably. "Well, since my grandfather left me this house, the newspaper, and some farmland out west of town, he felt he had to parcel out his personal belongings to the other members of the family. By the time my aunts, uncles, and cousins had claimed their share of the furniture, this was all that was left. So far, I've sunk all my money into updating the newspaper, and there's been nothing left to spend on the house."

They passed on through a roomy, high-ceilinged kitchen and out onto a screened-in porch. There in a cardboard box squirmed four bits of puppy fluff only a few weeks old.

"They're adorable, Sadie," Erica cooed as she knelt and picked up a solid-black puppy. He wagged his thread of a tail and tried to lick her cheek. Erica smiled over at Jed. "Did you inherit them, too?"

He sighed. "Not exactly. A very pregnant Sadie was dumped out on the square about a month ago. It seems the animal overpopulation problem is as severe here as it is everywhere else in the country. Everyone felt sorry for her, but they already had all the pets they wanted. No one would take her in. Then, wouldn't you know it, she chose to have the pups in the alley behind the newspaper. When I found them, I couldn't stand it any longer. The guilt was too much. I loaded them all up and brought them home."

"But if the situation's that critical, how will you get rid of five dogs?"

He shrugged. "I may just have to keep them all. But for sure, Sadie and her daughters are getting spayed as soon as the vet gives the okay."

Erica eyed him skeptically. "You'd actually consider keeping five dogs?"

"Sure. What other choice do I have?"

"That's very generous of you."

"Yeah, I know," he said sarcastically. "I'm a prince among men. Either that or the chump of the century."

Erica felt a stab of tenderness. "Well, I vote for the prince theory."

"Thanks." The undercurrent of emotion was there between them again. He reached a hand down to her. She put the puppy back and let him pull her to her feet—and straight into the circle of his arms.

She could feel her heart thudding erratically in her chest. When she looked up at him, the light smoldering in his eyes began to have a hypnotic effect on her. She found she had no desire to protest as he held her close and lowered his lips to hers. She stood as if paralyzed, at once enjoying the sweet sensation of being pressed against his solid frame, yet still maintaining a curious emotional detachment.

Jed Daniels was good at pleasing women, however. And as the kiss grew more fervent, she felt the two facets of herself melding dangerously into one. The detachment was fading, and fires were being stirred. An alarm bell clanged loudly in her brain. It was happening—the thing she'd vowed only hours ago to control. She'd given in to the pull of her emotions. Without a wife looming between them, Erica had no real compelling reason to keep her distance. Or did she?

What about the threat he posed to her mission? What about the fact that in two weeks she'd be back in New York, and Willow Springs, Oklahoma would be a rapidly fading memory? This had to stop!

She pushed against him, but he held her fast. And once again she saw that irritating pinprick of humor dancing in his eyes.

"What's wrong, Miss Stone? Is a romantic interlude not in your battle plan?"

"Precisely." She was at once disillusioned and grateful that he'd reminded her of this perverse side of his nature. "Nor should it be in yours." She wrenched free. "Exactly what type of game are you playing, anyway?"

"Game?" he asked with exaggerated innocence. "What makes you think this is a game?" His eyes smoldered again. "I'm dead serious. I've never felt this strong an attraction to anyone before. Have you?"

Granted, "strong attraction" might even be an understatement as far as her feelings were concerned. But Erica wasn't about to admit that to him.

"Surely you don't deny the chemistry between us?" he prodded.

"No, I don't deny it. But I suspect there's some other reason behind this playboy pursuit you've mounted. Why don't we get the ulterior motives out in the open? It will be easier to determine the winner if we both know the rules of the game."

He raised an eyebrow. "You aren't much for intrigue, are you?"

"Intrigue and psychological maneuvering waste time and energy. I've never gone in for them."

"Neither have I," Jed conceded with a grin. "But I thought perhaps I should alter my tactics in dealing with the big-city wheeler-dealers."

"And romancing the company representative is part of your new strategy?"

"No." He sobered. "That wasn't part of my original plan. It just happened. There's a lot more going on between us than I ever bargained for."

"But you weren't above trying to use that once you realized it existed."

"Nor were you," he challenged. "Otherwise you wouldn't have come into my office looking so feminine and desirable."

That wasn't exactly true, but it was close, Erica had to admit. She'd plotted *before* the fact, and he *after*. Little difference.

"I notice you're not denying the charge, Miss Stone," he taunted.

She shrugged. "Why should I? I was hoping to charm you into changing your stand. There's nothing wrong with that."

His eyes smoldered provocatively again. "No, there isn't. In fact, it still might work. Want to give it a try?" He reached for her playfully.

"No way." She stepped deftly out of his reach. "You're not getting off the hook that easily. Now it's your turn to confess. Somehow I think your strategy was a bit more convoluted than mine. For instance, what was the rationale behind all those speaking engagements you so cleverly set up? Those can't do anything other than help my cause."

"And mine, too. My editorials can only go so far in convincing people to vote the right way. And since I can't take time to go around and buttonhole each stockholder individually, this will give me a forum to speak to whole groups of them at one time. Surely you realize all either of us can do is present the facts and trust people to make the right decision."

It sounded reasonable. Too reasonable!

He had to have more up his sleeve than that. By arranging the debates, he was giving her a fifty-fifty chance to win.

Only a fool gave an opponent such an even break, and somehow Jed Daniels did not impress her as a fool.

She tried once more to draw him out. "Suppose I win the debates, and the people decide to vote in favor of the sale?"

He smiled slowly. "I guess that's a risk I'll just have to take."

The words were spoken in a completely neutral tone, but Erica could tell he didn't consider it a risk at all. Her spine stiffened with a new resolve. She was determined to wipe that arrogant smile off his face if it was the last thing she ever did. "Well, Mr. Daniels, it looks like we're headed into round two. And I'd like to remind you, the arena is that of your choosing."

"So noted. And under the circumstances, I think it would help the overall tone of the matter if you would call me Jed."

"Very well... Jed," she said coolly. "Now, I really must go. If you'll remember, I have an editorial to write for your paper tomorrow."

Chapter Four

"... And the woman in the third row wearing the flowered dress makes the most beautiful hand-sewn quilts you'd ever hope to see," Jed proclaimed.

Erica glowered at him. They were seated on the platform waiting to address the Ladies Auxiliary. The call asking her to speak had come as a result of her first editorial in yesterday's newspaper.

Jed had arrived shortly after she did. And from the moment he'd taken his seat beside her, he'd been babbling inanely about various members of the audience. For what purpose, she couldn't imagine—unless it was to distract her and make her nervous. In which case, he was succeeding remarkably well.

"Will you be quiet," she snapped. "I'm reviewing my opening statement."

"Relax," he teased. "This isn't a trial."

"Oh, isn't it?" she retorted, pulling yet another report from her briefcase. When Jed shrugged and turned his attention to his own set of crumpled notes, Erica made a great show of shuffling through the neat sheaf of papers on the table in front of her. She knew the material by heart, of course. But she was simply in no mood to play games with Jed Daniels—at least until she came up with an angle that gave her an equal chance of winning.

She felt very uneasy looking out over the group. The focus of her campaign, she had already decided, should be to develop a relationship of trust with the townspeople. Which might be harder than she anticipated. These women were looking at her with a mixture of awe and suspicion—thanks mostly, she was sure, to Jed's smear campaign. She'd lost their support even before she had a chance to present her case, unless. . . .

Unless she could demonstrate in some tangible way that she and her company really were interested in them and their town and their personal lives.

And she might be able to turn the tables on Jed Daniels in the process!

She straightened her papers very deliberately for a final time, removed her glasses, and turned to him with what she hoped was a bewitching smile. "Now, Jed, what were you saying about that lovely woman and her quilts?"

He regarded her warily. "I thought you weren't interested."

She did her best to sound innocent. "Whatever gave you that idea?"

He clearly thought she'd lost her mind. "Her name is Thelma Hanks, and she . . . uh . . . makes hand-sewn quilts in all the traditional patterns."

"Well, now, isn't that wonderful. And what about that young red-haired woman sitting next to her—anything unusual about her?"

"That's Thelma's granddaughter, Rachel Yates. She has a set of red-haired twins. Girls, about three years old now, I guess. You may have noticed them at the town picnic the other night."

She hadn't, of course, but Erica recognized the information as potentially useful. Before she could pump him for anything more, however, the meeting was called to order. She'd just have to make do with what she'd learned.

Erica spoke first. She was acutely aware that her material was pretty dry and unappealing—particularly for an audience of housewives. But she smiled sweetly and made eye contact with each woman in turn. It seemed to be working. She could sense them warming to her. If she played her cards right, maybe she could still win them over. She finished feeling more or less positive about her effort.

Until Jed took the floor.

He was poised, witty, charming. Erica couldn't believe the star-struck expressions that settled on the women's faces. They were staring at him like he was a rock star and they were mindless teenage groupies. Apparently he wasn't above capitalizing shamelessly on his blatant sex appeal.

But he wasn't entirely to blame. Erica held the audience partially responsible. Granted, he was handsome, and granted his voice was resonant and soothing, and granted those ice blue eyes could set any red-blooded female's heart racing. But this was ridiculous. Why, they were so busy gawking, they probably weren't hearing a word he said.

Oh, well, at least when they surfaced, the only facts they'd remember were those she'd given them. Now, had they been asked to describe Jed's appearance, that might be a different matter. They'd all surely noticed that his eyes were the exact blue of a cloudless summer sky, and how that errant lock of wheat-colored hair was forever falling down over his forehead, and the way that crisp navy blazer hugged his broad shoulders. . . .

Good grief! She gave herself a sharp mental shake. She was falling under his spell as surely as these hapless women.

With great difficulty, she forced herself to pay attention. It was essential that she knew the charges he was making so she could mount an effective defense.

Jed's statements weren't particularly inflammatory or insulting, she found. He just kept stressing the need for caution and questioning the commitment an out-of-state firm would have for the community. If he raised no more serious objections than these, he was playing right into her hands. All she had to do was convince the townspeople that her company was sincere and concerned for their best interests. Which fit right into the plan she'd concocted earlier. Now, if she just played her cards right....

And, unknowingly, Jed himself may have dealt her the winning hand.

Her gaze settled on Thelma Hanks and her pretty young granddaughter. She didn't have much ammunition to fight with at this point, but it would have to do. Again she wished she'd paid more attention to Jed's babblings.

When Jed finished, there were a surprising number of relevant questions. So evidently the women had absorbed some of what he'd said. With an unnerving jolt, it occurred to Erica that her evaluation of the audience's reaction to him might be colored by a proprietary haze of jealousy. She simply hadn't wanted to admit to her own discomfort at watching other women watch him. But maybe that *had* entered in....

Don't be ridiculous! she reprimanded herself. She was above allowing her emotions to interfere with her objectivity. Besides, she had no claim on Jed Daniels. Nor did she want one. He was the enemy. Still, she couldn't quite shake the memory of that disturbing kiss they'd shared after the picnic.

Decision of the Heart

Thankfully, a volley of questions directed at her forced her to focus once more on the situation at hand. It was all she could do to ignore Jed's presence as she joined him at the podium to answer. Her irritation with him quickly overshadowed the pull of physical attraction between them. Instead of returning to his seat so she could have a turn unhindered, he just stood there, so close their arms were touching, smiling that beguiling smile.

She moved in closer and gave him a sharp jab to the ribs with her elbow, but he still wouldn't budge. Oh, well, let him pull his petty little pranks. She'd get even soon enough.

Finally all questions were answered to the audience's satisfaction, and the meeting was dismissed. Erica quickly stuffed her notes into her briefcase, and left the stage. She did her best to appear nonchalant as she bore down upon Thelma Hanks and her red-haired granddaughter.

"Thank you ladies for coming," she said brightly as she passed them. She took another step to achieve just the right touch of spontaneity before turning back to them. "Say," she said casually to Rachel, "you were at the picnic, weren't you, with a pair of little twin girls?"

The young woman was obviously flattered to think she'd been noticed. "Why, yes. Those are my babies, Beth and Tracey."

"Well, they're just *darling*," Erica cooed. She felt a sudden stab of conscience. She'd never resorted to such deceptive methods before. But, she rationalized, she hadn't lied. She hadn't actually said she'd seen Rachel or the twins. She'd merely commented on the fact that they'd all been at the picnic and that the little girls were darling. And she was sure both statements were true. It went without saying that all children were darling.

Rachel was practically beaming now, as was everyone around who'd heard the exchange. Which was exactly the result Erica had hoped for. She'd just scored big in the battle toward establishing a warm, caring image. She moved in for the kill. "I'm Erica Stone," she said, offering her hand to Rachel.

"I'm Rachel Yates, and this is my grandmother, Thelma Hanks."

"Thelma Hanks," Erica mused as she shook the woman's hand. "Your name sounds so familiar. Now, what have I heard about you? Oh, yes! That you make the most beautiful quilts in the area."

Thelma wasn't as easily snowed as Rachel had been. She eyed Erica warily. "And just where did you hear that, young lady?"

Erica blanched. This was getting more complicated. No wonder she didn't like using such tactics. There seemed no way out of this now except to lie, or allow the conversation to turn in a direction she didn't want it to go—straight back to Jed Daniels.

Before she could decide which was worse, Jed appeared at her elbow and took the matter neatly out of her hands. "She heard it from me, Thelma." He winked flirtatiously at the old woman. "You know how I'm always bragging about your quilts."

Thelma tittered girlishly. "Now, Jed, lots of people around here quilt."

"But none of them have won the grand prize at the county fair for five years straight," Jed cajoled. "What pattern are you entering this year?"

Thelma launched excitedly into her dilemma about whether to sew the wedding ring pattern or go with her old

Decision of the Heart 51

standby, the log cabin. Rachel and the other women quickly chimed in with suggestions, and the debate was on. A debate that neatly froze Erica out of the conversation.

And there was Jed right in the middle of the group, acting like the topic ranked among his favorites—right up there with baseball and hockey. Darn him anyway! Erica was furious with him for horning in. He'd managed to thwart her plan and wrap the women neatly around his little finger in the process. They were hanging on his every word. Like he knew anything about quilts in the first place!

But she was too much of a competitor to be displaced so easily. She elbowed past Jed, managing to give him another jab to the ribs as she did so, and smiled sweetly at Thelma. "I'd love to see some of your work, Mrs. Hanks. I'm always in the market for handmade linens."

"You mean you want to buy one of my quilts?" Thelma's distrust seemed to melt away, Erica noticed, at the prospect of making some cold hard cash.

She pressed her advantage. "Of course. If you'll give me directions to your house, I can drop by in the next few days."

"I live way out in the boonies. You'd never find the place," Thelma scoffed rather rudely.

"I'll bring her," Jed offered benignly. "In fact, Thelma, we'll be halfway to your place when we go speak to the Rotary Club tomorrow."

Rotary Club? This was the first Erica had heard of speaking to the Rotary Club.

Jed flashed her an innocent smile. "I got the call just before I came over here today. I took the liberty of accepting for both of us."

He was taking a lot of liberties, Erica fumed silently,

noticing that he'd prudently stepped back out of elbow range.

"The Rotary Club meets for lunch out at that restaurant on the interstate highway, don't they?" Thelma mused. "You're right, Jed. You might as well run on out to my farm from there."

"Good." Jed looked pleased with himself. "We'll be there about the middle of the afternoon then."

Erica felt like screaming. The last thing she wanted was to spend the day with Jed Daniels. At the moment she literally loathed the man. She spoke up forcibly. "I don't want to inconvenience you, Mr. Daniels. I'll bring my car to the meeting, and you can give me directions."

"Oh, it's no trouble at all," Jed said expansively.

"Besides, I already told you, you'd just get lost," Thelma proclaimed impatiently. "Let Jed bring you." She gave him another shy smile. "I'll look forward to seeing you tomorrow, Jed."

He winked. "I'll look forward to seeing you, too. Think you can come up with a pan of your famous brownies for me?"

"You betcha." Thelma winked back. "Well, guess I'd better skedaddle. Got cows to milk and chickens to feed. You coming, Rachel?"

"Yes, grandmother." Rachel smiled warmly at Erica. " 'Bye, Miss Stone."

The rest of the women rapidly bid them farewell, and Erica was at last alone with Jed. She turned on him angrily. "What's the big idea of going ahead with all those arrangements against my wishes?"

Jed's eyes twinkled provocatively. "Just trying to help."

"Yeah, sure! Well, I don't want *or need* your help!"

Decision of the Heart   53

"Now, now. You'd better wait to make such statements till we're back safely from Thelma's. Her place is pretty remote, and you wouldn't want me to leave you stranded in the wilderness, would you?"

Erica wasn't fooled by his affable tone. There was a veiled threat in there somewhere. Somehow he knew what she'd been up to. And he knew that she knew that he knew. Furthermore, he knew there was no way she could confront him about his underhanded plotting without revealing her own. The game was growing more complicated by the moment.

And clearly he'd won another round.

"Oh, Mrs. Hanks, these are lovely!" Erica's words of praise were sincere as she examined Thelma's quilts the next afternoon.

"Why, thank you. I enjoyed making each and every one of them."

On the drive out, Erica had come up with several carefully couched compliments to offer in case Thelma's quilts had proven a disappointment. But the design and workmanship were exceptional on all the dozen or so examples spread out across the furniture in the rustic little living room.

Erica was having a hard time choosing. She finally narrowed it to two—one in exquisite blues and greens, and one in shades of rust and yellow. She really wanted both, providing the cost wasn't too great.

Her mind made up, she turned to Thelma. "How much?"

The old woman grew thoughtful. "I don't rightly know. I ain't never sold one of my quilts before. I usually just give them away as wedding gifts and such. But there's a lot of work involved. . . ."

Erica steeled herself for an outrageous price. At various craft shows, she'd seen quilts no prettier than these priced at several hundred dollars.

Thelma's sharp little eyes came into focus again. "How about a hundred?"

"But, Mrs. Hanks, you can't mean—"

"Too much, huh?" Thelma interrupted. "How about fifty then?"

Erica laughed. "What I started to say is that you shouldn't sell them so cheaply. If you took them into Oklahoma City to a good craft shop, you could easily get much more."

"That so? Then I might look into doing that. But the price still stands for you. You can have any of 'em for a hundred dollars."

"Well, I want these two." Erica indicated her choices. "And I'll pay you two hundred each, and not a penny less."

Thelma shrugged. "That's fine by me. They don't cost me nothing but my time. Other folks give me their leftover material after they cut out their dress patterns and such."

"You mean these quilts were pieced from scraps of material? Then they really are works of art. Most quilters today buy new material so they can come up with pleasing color combinations."

"Poppycock! That'd be too easy. It'd take away all the challenge."

Erica laughed as she made out her check. Thelma was a true artisan of the old school. There weren't many like her around anymore.

Jed had been standing quietly by munching on a brownie during the exchange. He now wiped his fingers on a napkin and helped Thelma fold the quilts and stuff them in grocery bags.

Decision of the Heart

"If you want, Jed, I can wrap up the rest of the brownies for you to take with you," Thelma offered.

"What a sweetheart!" Jed grabbed the woman and planted a smacking kiss on her cheek. "My long-standing proposal of marriage is still open."

"Oh, you!" Thelma cried with a girlish giggle. Blushing, she fought her way free and headed toward the kitchen to pack up the brownies.

Erica could only marvel. She had a feeling that no woman of any age could withstand Jed's charms should he decide to seriously apply them. A dangerous light flared into his eyes when he caught her watching him, and a warning bell clanged loudly in her brain. It suddenly occurred to her that she might even have to include herself in that number.

It was a frightening admission. She had to keep such traitorous thoughts at bay. The man was merely human, after all, with no magical powers to overwhelm her will. She *could* resist. She *would* resist.

There. The matter was settled once again.

Nevertheless, Erica sat as close as possible to the passenger side door of Jed's station wagon as they left Thelma's remote little farm and bounced along the rutted dirt track back toward civilization. Erica tried to ignore the sensual pull between them by reviewing the events of the day.

Her speech before the Rotary Club had gone much better than the one to the Ladies Auxiliary. For one thing, the audience had been mostly men, so Jed had lost the advantage his drop-dead good looks gave him with females. She'd come away feeling she'd made a good showing.

The diner out on the interstate where the meeting was held had been a welcome surprise also. Crowded with travelers, it had a bustling urban flavor that made Erica homesick for the faster pace of New York.

They'd left immediately after the meeting for Thelma's, and Erica had indeed been glad she hadn't tried to find the place on her own. It was on across the interstate, several miles out in the country over twisting, unmarked dirt roads. She'd been hopelessly turned around from the beginning, and even now had no idea in which direction they were traveling. As much as she hated to admit it, she was lucky Jed had tricked her into allowing him to bring her. She supposed, in all fairness, she should tell him so.

Reluctantly, she looked over at him. "Thanks for driving me out."

"Sure." He smiled his sexy smile and patted the parcel on the seat beside him. "I had to get my brownies anyway." The light in his eyes sent a tingle down to her toes. "So, what are your plans for the quilts?"

Erica thought it strange that he was interested, but she answered anyway. "The blue one will look great in my bedroom. I may even get some pillow shams and use it as a spread. Then I have an antique quilt rack in my guest bedroom where I can display the other one."

"So you really did like them?"

"Of course. Couldn't you tell by the way I was carrying on?"

He shrugged. "I thought maybe you were putting on an act."

"An act! Why would I put on an act? And more to the point, if I were only acting, why would I buy something I didn't like?"

"As a sort of bribe. You know, to get Thelma to vote for the sale."

Erica bristled. "If you thought that, why were you willing to drive me out to her house?"

"Because Thelma needs the money, and I knew her vote wasn't for sale. And if you thought it was, you needed to learn your lesson early on."

"And you wanted to be there when I learned it, huh? You must not think very highly of me if you think I'd run around trying to buy votes."

"Well, maybe 'buy' is too strong a word. But it sure can't hurt your cause to flash a lot of cash around and let it be known there's more where that came from if the big city people move into Willow Springs."

"But that's true!" Erica protested. "And why is it bad? If my company buys the plant, there *will* be a better cash flow in the community. Immediately, when the new management people arrive and start buying houses and goods. And in the future, when the profits increase and employees' salaries go up."

"I've heard all that before, and it just sounds too good—"

"—to be true. Yeah, yeah. I know." Erica crossed her arms and glared at him defiantly. "You're a very suspicious man, Jed Daniels!"

He grinned his infuriating grin. "Don't act innocent with me, Erica Stone. I had every right to be suspicious. You were making some pretty smooth moves yesterday when you pumped me for information, then used it to home in on Thelma and Rachel like a missile after an enemy bomber."

She winced. She'd left herself wide open for that one. "Well, you forced me into it," she retorted. "You've painted us as uncaring outsiders. And as the visible representative of Ledbetter Enterprises, I was trying to prove that the company *is* interested in the personal welfare of the citizens."

"By lying?" he exclaimed.

"I didn't lie! Not once!"

"Well, you certainly bent the truth all out of shape with that line you were feeding Rachel. 'Your twins are just darling,' " he mimicked in a derisive falsetto voice.

Erica glowered more fiercely. "Well, they *are* darling, aren't they?"

"Of course, but—"

"But nothing! See? I didn't lie! And what about you—up there at that podium, working those women like a gigolo! Don't tell me all those moonstruck expressions happened by accident. You didn't behave all that honorably with Thelma, either. Maybe her vote can't be bought, but it might well be *charmed*. And you laid it on pretty thick, both yesterday and today. Also, you were up to something sneaky by telling me the life history of every member of the Ladies Auxiliary. I just haven't figured out what it was yet."

"Now, just a cotton-picking minute!" He took his eyes off the road to glower back. "I was only trying to show you there's a human side to this business deal you're concocting. I wanted to translate those cold, impersonal statistics rattling around in your head into flesh-and-blood people. If you see anything sinister in that—" He broke off abruptly and a slow smile spread across his face. "It just occurred to me that we both were dabbling in intrigue again, and we've already recognized that neither of us is that good at it. What say we declare a truce? I'm sorry for my part."

Erica was startled by his sudden candor. He continued to amaze her. Reluctantly, she admitted he was right. And she saw no purpose in extending what amounted to a childish show of temper. "Okay, I'm sorry, too."

The interstate highway came into sight then, and Jed turned to her unexpectedly. "Hey, want to stop by the diner for a cup of coffee?"

"Yeah, that might be nice," she answered impulsively. She instantly regretted her decision. So far in this encounter, they were even. Prolonging the skirmish would only benefit him, not her. She opened her mouth to announce she'd changed her mind, but that spark of challenge was back in his eyes. He was daring her again, and somehow she couldn't bring herself to back down. She stubbornly stared out the window, cursing her competitive nature. What was she anyway, a masochist?

The time she spent with Jed was an emotional roller-coaster ride—exciting, but with an element of potential danger that kept her heart in her throat. She didn't need that type of excitement. She'd never gone in for amusement park rides; she'd always considered them nothing but a cheap thrill.

She ventured a glance at Jed and revised her simplistic analogy. Associating with him might be thrilling and even a little dangerous. But never cheap. If she let him get too close, she knew it would cost her dearly.

And it was a price she wasn't willing to pay.

Chapter Five

A few minutes later Erica was seated across from Jed in a secluded corner booth of the diner, more sorry than ever that she'd come. Those blue eyes were boring into hers in a way that set her heart hammering against her rib cage. She was glad when the waitress appeared with their coffee. It gave her an excuse to shift her gaze from his on the pretense of studying the activity going on around them.

The diner was again bustling with travelers, and the harried staff was too busy to take any special notice of them. It was a relief not to have all eyes focused on her, as had been the case since she'd arrived in Willow Springs. She realized that it was only natural that the townspeople be curious about her, but it triggered too many bad memories of her childhood . . . and reminded her of why she liked the big city. There she could remain as anonymous as she pleased.

"It's a little livelier here than in town," Jed said shrewdly, as if he'd guessed her thoughts. "I suppose you prefer a faster pace."

"Yes, I do. I'll admit, Willow Springs does take some getting used to." She stopped abruptly. She'd inadvertently allowed her disdain for small towns to creep into her voice. She quickly changed the subject. "Have any other organizations contacted you about speaking?"

"A couple." He appeared suspicious about the shift in

Decision of the Heart

topics, but let it drop. "At this point, though, we can't wait for them to come to us." He pulled a sheet of paper from his pocket and slid it across the table toward her. "I had my assistant editor, Lucille Faraday, go through the community calendar and make a list of all the clubs scheduled to meet before the vote. I can wangle invitations to nearly all of them if you're agreeable."

"Why wouldn't I be agreeable?"

"You weren't too happy yesterday when I told you about the Rotary Club."

"That's because you acted so high-handed when you sprang it on me."

"I figured as much. That's why I decided to check with you beforehand."

"That's very big of you." Sarcasm again. She needed to watch that. Jed wouldn't tolerate too much backtalk. And she really was grateful they might be able to speak to the dozen or so groups he had listed. "You really think we can address all of these?"

"Sure. With a little friendly arm twisting, that is. You game?"

"Of course." She looked at the first club on the list. "So, I should be ready to speak to the Moose Lodge tomorrow night, huh?"

"Oh, yeah. That's a sure thing. The president's an old fishing buddy."

"And I suppose you have similar contacts in all these other groups?"

"Pretty much. Contacts are vital in the newspaper business."

In any business, Erica thought wryly. And she'd bet Jed Daniels was as skillful at cultivating them as any of B.J.'s highly paid lobbyists. Maybe even more so because of his subtle charm. She was lucky that, for whatever obscure reason, he had decided to let her benefit from his connections. She just wished she had some idea of what he was up to.

His background might give her a clue of where he was coming from. "Mind if I ask you a question?" she ventured.

He grinned provocatively. "Not at all. Go ahead."

"What are you doing here in Willow Springs? You're obviously talented enough to work for a much larger newspaper."

"Oh, I did—once. I got a job at the *Daily Oklahoman* in Oklahoma City straight out of journalism school. From there I went to the *Chicago Tribune*."

"The *Trib*, huh? I'm impressed. What made you leave?"

"About five years ago, my grandfather asked me to come and help him with the *Gazette*. His health was failing, and I was the only one of his offspring who had any interest in the newspaper game."

"And you jumped at the chance to return to the old hometown."

Jed chuckled. "Are you kidding? In the first place, Willow Springs isn't my hometown. I was raised in Oklahoma City. My parents still live there, as a matter of fact. I always thought of Willow Springs as a boring little burg, and I hated the idea of being marooned out here in the sticks. You said you were impressed with my working at the *Trib*. Well, let me tell you, you couldn't be a fraction as impressed as I was. Man, I saw that as one giant step up the career ladder heading straight toward the *Washington Post* or the *New York Times*."

"Then why give it up and come back here?"

"Some decisions you make with your heart, not your

head. Even though common sense tells you it's a mistake and it goes against everything you ever thought you wanted, you somehow know it's the right thing to do. This was one of those decisions. My grandfather needed me. I loved that old man, maybe even more than I love my parents. Everything I am—all my basic drives—I inherited from him. He was my hero. I couldn't say no to him. So I quit and moved back here a year or so before he died to help him out.''

"It would seem enough that you devoted a whole year to keeping him happy. Why didn't you get on with your life after he died?"

"I tried, believe me. But I couldn't find a buyer who wanted a financially ailing newspaper with outdated equipment and a staff of senior citizens."

"You could've just shut it down," Erica pointed out.

"Yeah, that's what my family wanted me to do. But when it came down to the wire, I just couldn't do it. It would've meant burying my grandfather's dreams along with his body. He believed small-town free enterprise was the backbone of America. He always said people in rural communities shouldn't be forced to look to the big cities for the necessities of life, and that included the news. The *Daily Oklahoman* isn't going to care if Will Harris' garage gets robbed, or if Rachel Yates delivers twins—"

"—or if Ledbetter Enterprises gobbles up Lawn Magic Mowers."

He grinned at her. "Precisely. And so, rather unwillingly, I took up the cause. But it was hard to say good-bye to life in the fast lane."

"Then why did you? I understand your initial reaction of wanting to carry on for your grandfather. But noble as it sounds, it's not sufficient reason to keep you here for five years. Nobody's that self-sacrificing. So come clean. Why are you still here?''

His grin broadened. ''You would've made a good journalist yourself. Dig until you get the story behind the story, right? I guess I stay for the satisfaction. Putting the *Gazette* back on its feet against all odds was immensely satisfying. And so was showing the townspeople they still have something to offer the world. They needed to believe in themselves again. They needed someone to tell them they could revitalize their town and their individual businesses if they just didn't cave in to the pressures of modern society. There's still a place—and even a hunger—for the life-style small towns can provide.''

Erica remembered Allan's wistful longing for such a life, and knew Jed was right. It just wasn't for everyone—*namely her*. ''You sound like a one-man chamber of commerce,'' she said mockingly.

''I suppose I do. But it takes just that type of cheerleading to inspire people to try.'' Luckily Jed was too intent on expounding his theories to notice her tone of voice. ''Take the employees of the *Gazette*. They're capable of producing a newspaper as slick as the *Daily Oklahoman* because of their cumulative experience. I'm trying to show them that.''

''You act as if it's a difficult thing to do.''

He grimaced. ''It is. My grandfather was pretty autocratic. He didn't much believe in delegating responsibility. Consequently, the employees lack the self-confidence to take the initiative and act on their own. Lately I've purposefully been disappearing at critical times during the day so they'll have to make a few decisions on their own.''

Jed's description of his grandfather brought to mind Erica's inital misconception of ''Daniels the Dinosaur.'' She'd just missed the right Daniels by a generation or two. She suddenly had a sneaking suspicion. "Was your grandfather's name by any chance Jedidiah?"

"As a matter of fact it was. It's the name every firstborn son of the Daniels clan has been saddled with for several generations now. As a kid, I hated it. But since then, I've grown to accept it as a badge of honor—the perpetuation of a family tradition. A tradition that will continue with my son."

Why did the idea of Jed with a son intrigue her so? Erica wondered. The answer sprang immediately to mind. Because that son would need a mother, and she was sorely tempted to volunteer for the job. Good grief! Where had that thought come from? Left field, obviously. She chased it back there with dedicated fervor. No doubt it was that infernal physical attraction kicking in again. She stirred her coffee vigorously and avoided eye contact with Jed. If he read these thoughts as aptly as he had her others, she was in real trouble.

However, when she dared glance at him, he was waving at an elderly couple across the room. The pair was sipping coffee and watching them intently.

"Who's that?" she asked nervously.

"Ollie and Melba Underwood. They run the hardware store in town."

Something in the couple's expressions told Erica that she and Jed had been under surveillance for some time. She'd learned years ago to recognize ardent rumormongers, and the Underwoods fit the bill perfectly. So much for thinking the diner was a safe refuge from the small-town mania for gossip.

Jed was eyeing her curiously. "What's wrong?"

"It makes me uncomfortable to have people watch me like that. I hate being the center of attention."

He seemed amused. "Doesn't it go with the territory in your position?"

"But I want the attention directed to the business deals I'm negotiating, not my personal life."

Jed laughed. "It's hard to separate the two in a town this size."

Yes, tell me about it! Erica thought ruefully.

"Speaking of your personal life," Jed continued flirtatiously, "that's a subject I'd like to know more about. What do you do with your time when you're not gallivanting around the globe facilitating corporate buyouts?" He reached across the table and laid his hand over hers.

An electric current pulsed up her arm. Erica quickly pulled her hand away. He was actually egging the Underwoods on, if she were any judge. It irked her that he was taking all this so lightly. Rationally, she knew the prospect of a few petty rumors shouldn't bother her either. After all, they would have no lasting effect on her life—particularly considering the limited time she'd be in Willow Springs.

She squared her shoulders and answered Jed's question. "I go to craft fairs and travel into New England to shop for antiques."

"Antiques, huh? Any particular period?"

"Victorian, mostly. I find that era so enchanting. I recently bought a new apartment, and I'm trying to get it furnished before winter."

"So you can curl up in front of the fire with a good book ... or with the man of your dreams?"

"The good book part is more accurate," she said coolly.

"I'm just too busy to become involved seriously with anyone."

His eyes clouded. "Ah, yes. Your career again. It rather consumes you, doesn't it?"

"It's important to me, yes, but I wouldn't go that far. It's merely a means to finance the life-style I want, as it is with everyone else."

"And that life-style doesn't include a man?"

"Not at this point." This was getting too personal. She had no desire whatsoever to discuss her love life—or lack of one, actually—with Jed Daniels. She quickly changed the subject. "So, how are Sadie and the pups?"

Again it was obvious he wasn't fooled by her clumsy ploy. Nevertheless, he played along with her. "Sadie's fine, and the pups get more active each day. That black one you like is becoming a nervy little devil. He actually growled at me last night when I tried to pet him. I told him he'd better watch his step. After all, I'm the one who brings home the puppy chow."

Erica laughed in spite of herself. "I'll bet they're cute."

"They are. Pesky, but cute. I'll need to get a taller box in just a few days or they'll be climbing out and getting into all kinds of mischief."

"Maybe you should move them outside."

"I can't yet. The yard's not fenced and some strange dog might come along and hurt them. I've been meaning to get a fence built, but I don't have the money right now."

"I'd feel sorry for you if your poverty weren't self-imposed," she said cattily.

He lifted his cup in a mock salute. "Point well taken. And I wasn't really looking for sympathy. That's the last emotion I was hoping to arouse in you. . . ." Before she could come up with a suitable put-down, he continued. "Actually, I consider myself a lucky man. Since moving here, I've discovered life in the slow lane has definite perks, too. I wouldn't go back now even if I had the opportunity."

Erica tensed. This was, of course, where he would launch into the virtues of small-town living. No doubt the reasons he'd give would be poetic, but predictable. And she was in no mood for such drivel. "Please spare me the nonsense about golden sunsets, wading in crystal-clear streams, and awakening to the sound of birds singing," she said sarcastically.

He once more seemed amused. "Why? Such pleasures are too mundane for someone as sophisticated as you?"

"Not at all. You just need to keep in mind that the sun sets over the big city as well as the small town."

"Yeah, when you can see it through the smog."

"Look, Mr. Daniels, I'm here to buy a lawn mower plant—not buy into a way of life. You're making your sales pitch to the wrong person. I won't be involved at all here in Willow Springs once this deal is finalized."

Jed was no longer amused. "You sound like that can't be too soon for you," he said angrily.

Erica realized she'd allowed too much of her personal feelings to creep into her outburst. All she needed was to give him more ammunition for his smear campaign.

"I'm sorry," she said earnestly. "I know full well what a wonderful life-style you people enjoy here in Willow Springs. But I hope you're broad-minded enough to understand that what makes you happy might only make another person miserable."

"True." Jed's tone softened. "But that other person shouldn't be so sure this life-style wouldn't suit her until she's given it a try."

I have tried it! she wanted to scream at him. *For sixteen years I tried it. It was hell on earth, and I'll never go through that again!*

Erica took a long slow drink of coffee while she struggled to get her emotions under control. A man like Jed would never understand the insecurity that drove her. He sat across from her now so cocky and self-assured. There was obviously no painful ordeal in his past to haunt him. For whatever else Jed Daniels was, he was a man at peace—with himself, his surroundings, his life-style. He'd clearly found his niche in life. He was good for Willow Springs, and Willow Springs was good for him. Somehow that thought depressed her even further.

It took all the willpower she could muster, but when she looked up at him again, she even managed a stiff smile. "Like I said earlier, Jed, you're a one-man chamber of commerce. I'm glad you're so satisfied with your way of life. I didn't intend to offend you."

She meant every word, and he apparently recognized that. The anger faded completely from his eyes. "I'm sorry, too, for trying to foist my ideas off onto you. Forgive me?"

"Certainly." She gave a sigh of relief. Another disaster narrowly averted. Jed was appeased, and the Underwoods were seated far enough away that they hadn't overheard any of her careless talk. She knew they were watching, however. She could feel their beady eyes burning into her back.

She resented being in this situation, and she was angry with Jed for maneuvering her into it. He plainly enjoyed keeping her off-balance and at the mercy of her emotions. But she'd had enough. It was time to bring this encounter to a close.

Resolutely she drained her cup. "Well, Jed, shall we go?"

"Already? And here I had the impression you were enjoying my company."

"Oh, I was. And am. But it's time to get back down to business. We both have work to do to prepare for the next round." She consulted the list before slipping it into her purse. "The Moose Lodge, right?"

"Ah, yes." He sighed. "I forgot for a moment that we're foes. We could extend the truce into a permanent cease-fire, you know."

"There's too much at stake to give up the fight."

His gaze smoldered provocatively. "But it is tempting, isn't it?"

She decided to give him a taste of his own medicine and flirt back. "Yes, it's tempting. But big girls don't give in to temptation."

He lifted an eyebrow. "Oh, don't they?"

She bristled. "What do you mean by that?"

"The other night . . . at my house. You can't claim that was strictly business."

"A temporary lapse. It won't happen again."

"No? Wanna make a little wager on that?"

"Only fools gamble," she stated stiffly.

"Only cowards make claims they aren't ready to back up," he countered.

Erica knew he was reeling her in like a fish on a line, but she couldn't let the charge go unchallenged. "It's no idle claim, Mr. Daniels."

"Then prove it. Have dinner with me tomorrow night after we speak."

Dinner? That shouldn't be too bad, she thought. She'd

managed to hold her own here. With other people around. And a table between them. Dinner at a nice restaurant should prove no problem. "Okay. Where?"

"Does that make a difference?"

She shrugged. "I suppose not."

"Then at my place."

A tingle of fear crept up her spine, and she heard the unmistakable plop of a large fish (her) landing in a boat. The spark of challenge was back in his eyes. He thought he had her now, but she'd just show him! Now that she knew how sneaky and underhanded he was, she'd be ready for him. She didn't plan to get within ten feet of those tentacles he called arms. She gave herself a mental shake. Enough of the watery euphemisms. "I suppose your place would be all right. I'd like to see Sadie and the pups again."

"Only Sadie and the pups? Not me?"

"I've seen quite enough of you already."

He chuckled. "Oh, please. Stop with the flattery. It will go straight to my head." He picked up the check and slid out of the booth.

Erica felt a smooth surge of satisfaction as she followed him to the counter to pay. This skirmish had ended more or less in a tie. And tomorrow she'd deliver the final devastating blow to his oversized ego. If seduction was his aim, he'd be sorely disappointed. She repressed the niggling memory of similar plans she'd had yesterday to turn the tables on him. Just by the odds of sheer chance, though, it was time she came out the winner.

Her own words of moments ago came back to haunt her. Only fools gambled—particularly when the stakes were so high. She pushed the thought aside.

When they stepped out of the diner, Erica was surprised

to see clouds had gathered ominously overhead and a smattering of raindrops had begun to fall. "Where did this storm come from?" she exclaimed. "The sun was shining when we went inside not half an hour ago."

Jed laughed and set a brisk pace for the station wagon. "We have a saying here in Oklahoma. 'If you don't like the weather, wait a minute.' Storms sweep in and out in a matter of hours sometimes. In fact, the severe storms lab for the whole United States is located just a short distance away in Norman, Oklahoma."

"Severe storms? What kind of severe storms?"

"Wind, snow, sleet, hail. But mostly tornadoes." He opened the door for her. "Oklahoma has the distinction of being known as Tornado Alley."

"Great!" she muttered as she climbed into the car.

As Jed loped around to the driver's side, Erica noticed the Underwoods getting into an old blue sedan. Their smug expressions clearly said that they'd noted she and Jed were traveling together.

Jed didn't seem at all bothered. He even waved as they pulled past.

Erica felt a deepening dread. The rumors were sure to fly now. And they'd be even worse after she had dinner at Jed's house tomorrow night. That should set tongues wagging all over town.

She again saw the image of the poor fish flopping helplessly around in the bottom of the boat. She might as well accept her fate, and prepare to end up in the frying pan of public ridicule. And she had no one to blame but herself. Jed had dangled the bait, and she'd gone for it.

Hook, line, and sinker.

Chapter Six

Erica slept in the next morning. Not that she planned to. It just happened. The stress so far had taken its toll, and she was totally exhausted. It was almost noon before she bathed, dressed, and went downstairs.

Allan had agreed to have Junior pick him up and leave the car for her to use today. She wanted to call on the mayor at his office and start the ball rolling on plans for the final stockholders' meeting. The more people she could involve, the more theatrical and festive she could make the preparations, the better for her cause. People involved in the planning would naturally start to consider this their project, too, and would begin to help promote it. It was a subtle tactic that had worked well for her in the past, and hopefully it would work here as well.

She had some personal errands to run also, and a little advice from Hana might save her some valuable time. She stopped off in the dining room and snatched a doughnut and cup of coffee from the breakfast buffet before going in search of the landlady. She found Hana in the kitchen preparing meat loaf for the evening meal.

She perched on a stool by the counter and watched in fascination as the woman worked moist bread crumbs, tomato sauce, and spices into what must have been ten pounds of ground beef. "How'd you ever learn to cook in such huge proportions?" she asked with a grin.

"It takes more nerve than skill," Hana proclaimed as she divided the mixture into four loaves, one for each of the big round oak tables in the dining room. "You just got to plunge in and commit yourself to the effort. And there's no turning back once you tie up the money for this much meat. By the way, I got a group of new guests checking in later today. I'll put them at the other end of the hall from you, so you can have your privacy."

"Thanks. That's very nice of you."

"That's okay," Hana chuckled. "I know it ain't much fun sharing a bathroom with a bunch of grubby little kids. But when school's out in a few weeks, I'll be getting vacationing families in on a regular basis. The whole place will be full after that."

"Well, I'll be long gone by that time," Erica said wryly.

"Yep, that's right," Hana mused. "The days are sure slipping by, ain't they? I'll be sorry to see you go."

Erica knew she should say something about being just as sorry to leave, but she couldn't bring herself to tell an outright lie.

Hana was too busy with the meat loaves to notice her silence. "You gonna be here for supper tonight?" she asked absently.

"Afraid not. I'm scheduled to speak at the Moose Lodge."

"Well, those lodge meetings don't include dinner, so you better come down before you go and fix yourself a sandwich. Anytime you're hungry feel free to raid the refrigerator. I keep a ham baked all the time so I can fix a quick snack for boarders that check in at odd hours."

"That's good to know." Erica almost told Hana she wouldn't be taking her up on the offer tonight, thanks to Jed's dinner invitation. But she caught herself in time. The fewer people who knew, the better.

Mary entered the kitchen then, her arms loaded with dirty bed linen. She was obviously headed for the washing machine in the basement.

Hana waved her to a stop. "Say, Mary, I got a chance to cater a big barbecue next weekend. Will you be able to help me serve?"

"Sure," Mary answered eagerly. "Just remind me a few days ahead."

Erica watched as the girl disappeared down the basement steps. "She helps you cater in addition to working here? When does she have fun?"

"She don't!" Hana scowled. "It worries the daylights out of me, too. Poor kid. She don't have any friends her own age. She just goes to school and comes to work. This week school's out for spring break. All the other kids are out having a good time, but to Mary it's just a chance to work more hours and earn more money. That's some life for a young girl, huh?"

"Don't her parents object?"

"There's only her pa. And he's usually too drunk to object to anything. The worthless bum."

A cold chill ran down Erica's spine at the tone of Hana's voice. It mimicked so perfectly the harsh tone the adults in her childhood had used to describe her own father. So cold. So hard. So judgmental. They hadn't understood—hadn't wanted to understand—that her father drank to blot out his pain. Deliberately she pushed the memories away. She never allowed herself to dwell on what had happened all those years ago. . . .

But Hana wasn't ready to drop the subject of Mary's plight. "Yep, that poor girl supports herself completely, and she's even started a savings account for college. Some of her teachers are helping her apply for scholarships and such. I hope she makes it."

That sounded all too familiar, Erica thought bitterly. She and Mary had more in common than she'd ever imagined. "Well, at least she's got a couple of years yet for her savings to grow," she murmured.

"No, she don't. She skipped a couple of grades going through school. She'll be graduating about this time next year when she's sixteen."

Erica felt as though she were being forced to relive her own adolescence. She, too, had graduated at sixteen and gone off to college . . . never to look back. Her father had died soon after that, and his death had severed all ties to her hometown. The end of an era she rarely thought of anymore. And she wasn't going to start now. Determinedly she changed the subject. "Hana, where would I go in town to buy some shoes?"

Hana looked thoughtful. "I guess the Fashion Box would be the place. It's a real nice dress store, and it's got a shoe department. You won't find none of them fancy designer brands like you're used to, though."

Erica laughed. "That's okay. The fancy ones aren't proving very practical here in Willow Springs. I need some comfortable, low-heeled walking shoes so I can get around on days when Allan needs the car."

A sly grin spread over Hana's face. "You could save your money and let Jed drive you around. I heard he was more than happy to take you out to Thelma's farm . . . and then to the diner for a cup of coffee."

Erica battled her irritation and tried to sound casual as she replied. "News travels fast around here. You seem to know just how I spent my day yesterday. Mind telling me who told you?"

"Oh, I just heard it on the grapevine."

Erica was well acquainted with the small-town grapevine. She and her father had fallen victim to it often enough. She'd grown to hate those looks of pity folks had thrown her way as word of each of her father's binges, brawls, and blackouts made its way quickly around town. And the heartless teasing of the other children who'd overheard their parents' gossip was the hardest of all to bear.

"Well, how about it?" Hana prodded. "You got something going with Jed?"

"Of course not!" Erica insisted. "We simply stopped by the diner for a cup of coffee while we went over our speaking schedule, that's all."

Hana seemed immensely disappointed. "That's too bad. I was hoping you'd take my advice about getting in good with Jed."

Erica called on her dwindling reserve of patience. "Well, I've discovered there's a segment of townspeople who are on my side, and I decided it might be better to build on that support. Jed is firmly convinced he's right, and there seems no chance of changing his opinion."

"I don't know about that." Hana winked suggestively. "Seems like a pretty woman could find a way to change his mind . . . about a lot of things."

"Perhaps so, but this woman prefers to take a more direct approach. I'm too pressed for time to waste any trying to sweet-talk a stubborn man around to my way of thinking." She cut off any further discussion by glancing at her watch. "And speaking of wasting time, I'd better run along if I'm going shopping. Don't plan on me for lunch. I'll grab a bite downtown."

She pushed through the swinging door to the hallway before Hana could reply. The exchange with the landlady had really upset her. Although Hana obviously considered her insinuations nothing more than good-natured ribbing, Erica wasn't at all comfortable with the idea of people talking behind her back. And considering she'd almost reached the point of thinking of Hana as a friend, there was a definite edge of betrayal to the loose talk.

Oh, well. She should have known from past experience that it didn't pay to get too close to people like Hana. From here on out, it would be strictly business around the busybody landlady—and the rest of the townspeople as well. No more allowing Jed to goad her into doing things that could be taken the wrong way.

It was too late to get out of going to dinner with him tonight, but she'd be sure to avoid anything similar in the future. And perhaps she could still lessen the fallout from this obvious blunder. She'd stop by the *Gazette* and tell Jed she'd meet him somewhere instead of having him pick her up as they'd agreed yesterday. Hana and the Underwoods would love to get hold of a juicy tidbit of gossip like an intimate dinner for two at Jed's house. And he was just diabolical enough to tell Hana of their plans, unless Erica could eliminate his opportunity to do so.

She had another editorial ready anyway. Before this, she'd merely left the copy at the front counter. But maybe today she could manage a few words with Jed in private. It was her only option.

Even having made her decision, Erica found herself stalling as long as possible before actually going to the *Gazette*. First she stopped by the mayor's office, which was located in the surprisingly modern Town Hall across the square from the newspaper. Frank Ferris seemed remarkably glad to see her, and more than willing to help promote the sale. Erica considered that a major coup, and she knew B.J. would be thrilled. She set out on her shopping spree with a much more optimistic outlook.

She found her comfortable shoes—not one pair, but two, and even bought another pair of jeans and some blouses to supplement the ones Hana had loaned her. She ended up spending quite a bit of money at the clothing store, but didn't regret it. As Jed had inadvertently pointed out, it might help the townspeople see that outsiders would bring financial prosperity with them.

Finally, a little after five o'clock, Erica approached the newspaper just as the employees were leaving for the day. Her procrastination had served her well. Now there'd be fewer people present to complicate matters. Not everyone had left, however. As she pushed open the door to the lobby, she saw Jed deep in conversation with the two older women who worked in the outer office. With a grin, he came forward to greet her. She fixed him with a cold stare that caused the smile to melt comically and slide from his face.

"Good afternoon, Mr. Daniels," she said stiffly. "I have my next editorial here, and I need to speak to you privately about it."

The suspicious glint in his eyes told her he was having

quite a struggle about whether or not to play along with her. She intensified her glare.

He gave an almost imperceptible nod. "Certainly, Miss Stone. We can talk in my office." He motioned her around the partition.

She complied warily. Too late, she saw that he intended to take her arm. She had wanted to avoid physical contact at all costs. Her traitorous body responded of its own volition to his touch. Predictably, her pulse rate increased and her breathing grew more shallow. But again, short of making a scene, there was no way to escape his clutches.

"Before we get down to business, though," he said smugly, "I'd like you to meet my staff."

Erica gritted her teeth in frustration. Trust him to drag this out as long as possible. No doubt this was a further effort to force her to see the townspeople as human beings. The man never gave up.

He marched her over to the desk of one of the women, an attractive, sharp-eyed brunette in her late fifties. "This is my assistant editor, Lucille Farraday. She knows the nuts and bolts of this operation better than anyone, including myself. Needless to say, I couldn't do without her."

Lucille smiled knowingly. "I hope you'll remember that, boss, when it's time for my yearly evaluation. I could sure use a raise."

"Now, Lucille, you know sincere praise is more valuable than gold."

"Not at the grocery store, boss. There they only take cold hard cash. All that glib flattery sorta backfired on you, didn't it?" Lucille winked at Erica. "Has he tried the old charm on you yet, Miss Stone?"

Jed spoke up before Erica could reply. "Yes, I have,

Lucille. And unfortunately, she's as immune to it as you are." He turned Erica to face the other woman, who seemed to be fighting a smile. "And this is Madge Smith, Lucille's second-in-command. I could say a lot of nice things about her, too, but I don't dare considering I'm operating on a limited budget."

Madge glowered comically at Lucille. "See what you've done? Now Miss Stone will never know how valuable I am to this newspaper."

"You tell her, Madge," Jed urged as he steered Erica toward his office at the back of the building. "That will teach her to malign me in public."

At the last instant, to Erica's total dismay, he veered through the big double doors and into the pressroom. "One last person you have to meet," he insisted. Erica rolled her eyes in resignation and didn't resist as he bore down on a rotund elderly man walking thoughtfully around the now silent printing press.

Jed clapped the man on the back. "How'd today's print run go, George?"

"Pretty good, boss." George rubbed his chin. "I heard a strange rattle along toward the end of the day, though. Guess I'll pull off the housing and look things over a bit. Don't want her to go down during tomorrow's run."

"Sounds like a wise move," Jed said approvingly. "It's always better to stay on top of things like that. By the way, George, I'd like you to meet Miss Erica Stone. Erica, this is George Gilmore, the mechanical genius who keeps all this antiquated equipment purring like a kitten."

George nodded. "Howdy, Miss Stone. And my job ain't nearly so hard since the boss got those new modern parts to update the press."

"You're too modest, George," Jed insisted. "This place would fall apart without you, and we all know it."

Erica saw George's chest swell with pride. So Jed didn't ply his charms only on women. And grudgingly she admitted that so far when he'd bestowed praise, it had been justified, as in the case of Thelma's quilts. But all this had little to do with her reason for being here. She frowned impatiently up at Jed.

He cleared his throat. "Right. You wanted to speak to me privately. I'll check back with you later, George."

A young man appeared then from what was obviously the basement. He wore rubber gloves and a black plastic apron over a T-shirt and jeans.

"Hey, boss," he yelled. "Can you come down to the darkroom and look at this last batch of prints I developed?"

"Give me a couple of minutes, Pete. I need to speak to Miss Stone first." Jed grinned over his shoulder at Erica as she followed him into his office. "That's Pete Harvey, a high-school senior I'm training as a photographer. He's the hottest natural talent I've ever seen with a camera. I'd show you some of his work, but you don't seem anxious to hang around."

"You got that right," Erica said irritably, shutting the office door firmly behind her.

Jed reached for the manila envelope containing her editorial. "Well, let's see your copy. What kind of problem are you having with it?"

"None, actually. It's perfect. I needed an excuse to see you alone."

A teasing glint sprang into his eyes as he grabbed for her. "Ah.... So you've come around to my way of thinking at last."

Decision of the Heart

She slapped at his hands. "Will you stop that! That sort of thing can cause us both some very serious problems. And to avoid them, I think it's best if we meet somewhere tonight rather than you picking me up at the boardinghouse. If you won't agree to that, dinner is off."

His expression remained unchanged. "I suppose this has to do with your maniacal desire to avoid attention?"

She stiffened. He was obviously incapable of grasping how grave this matter was. "Exactly. And I resent you labeling it maniacal. I see no advantage to either of us in making a public display of our private lives."

"I see. Very well, you can meet me back here in an hour. The meeting's at seven, and we'll need a few minutes to drive out to the Lodge." He cast his eyes about warily and lowered his voice. "By the way, will I be able to recognize you?"

"Of course. Don't be ridiculous."

He shrugged. "Well, I thought you might show up in a false beard, trench coat, and dark glasses. I'll even leave the back door open so you can sneak in that way if you think it's necessary."

His teasing was growing more irritating by the minute. Apparently he never took anything seriously—including their battle over the sale. And that might just lead to his downfall. . . .

"As always, your thoughtfulness and concern for my wishes are overwhelming, Mr. Daniels," she said caustically. "But I'll be dressed normally, and I'll enter and leave by the front door."

"Suit yourself. I was just trying to get into the spirit of this cloak-and-dagger stuff. I guess I don't quite have the hang of it yet."

Bestowing her most venomous glare yet, Erica stalked out the door.

"I thought that went about as well as could be expected, didn't you?" Jed sounded annoyingly blasé about their presentation for the Moose Lodge.

Erica scowled over at him from where she sat, again pressed against the passenger-side door of his old station wagon as he guided the cumbersome car back toward town. Dinner still loomed in front of them. A lump rose in her throat. Why on earth had she agreed to go?

Jed didn't seem to notice her dark mood. "Aren't you the least bit curious about what I plan to feed you?" he teased.

She sighed. "No, I'm not curious. Undoubtedly at some point in your past you've taken gourmet cooking lessons from a European chef."

Jed laughed out loud. "Are you kidding? I'm lucky to even open a can of soup without a mishap. However, my kindly next-door neighbor has come to our rescue. The minute she heard I was entertaining a young lady, Mrs. Yosensky insisted on fixing supper for us and leaving it in my kitchen. It won't be anything fancy, but I can guarantee it will be good."

Oh, great! Erica thought. Now the neighbors were involved. Word of this dinner would be all over town by tomorrow. And she had no one to blame but herself. She'd agreed to this of her own free will. Sort of. She forced a weak smile. "That was very kind of Mrs. Yosensky."

"Yeah, the woman's a saint. Her husband died of cancer last spring, and now she's kind of at loose ends. She seems to have decided I need mothering, and I certainly have no complaints. She keeps me well supplied with home-cooked goodies."

"Thelma Hanks, Mrs. Yosensky.... How many other women do you have on the string who cater to your culinary needs?"

He lifted an eyebrow at the sarcasm in her voice. "Oh, the list goes on forever. There's only one drawback. They all have granddaughters, or nieces, or single young women from their churches they want to fix me up with."

"And I suppose you're such a confirmed bachelor you're not interested."

"Depends on the young woman. Every now and then I run into someone who interests me a lot." His sultry voice grated on her nerve endings. He was flirting with her again. Her breath caught at the tension that once more crackled between them. This dinner had been a very bad idea indeed!

She sat in silence as they wound through town to Jed's neat white house across from the park. As they pulled in the drive, a frail-looking little woman was coming down the front steps.

The woman waved and waited for them to get out of the car. "Howdy, Jed. I just left a plate of sandwiches, a pot of stew, and an apple pie on your kitchen counter. Hope you enjoy it."

Jed hugged the woman and kissed her on the cheek. "Mrs. Yosensky, you're a godsend. If you only knew how my stomach is growling right now."

His attentions caused the expected reaction. Mrs. Yosensky dissolved in a fit of girlish embarrassment. "I'm just happy to have an appreciative man around to cook for."

Erica forced her eyes away from the disgusting display. The man was impossible! If Mrs. Yosensky was a stockholder in Lawn Magic Mowers, this was another vote that would surely be cast for Jed's side of the issue.

Her brooding was interrupted as Jed turned to make introductions. "Mrs. Pearl Yosensky, I'd like you to meet my guest, Erica Stone."

"Well, isn't she a pretty little thing!" Mrs. Yosensky exclaimed as if Erica weren't even there. "Jed, you have good taste. I guess if my niece, Vera, can't have you, Erica is a good second choice."

Oh, pul-eeze! Erica snorted silently. The woman made it sound as though the "choosing" was all at Jed's discretion. She was tempted to retort that she wasn't all that enthusiastic about being the chosen one. But she knew that if she raised any objection it would only prolong this conversation and ultimately the whole evening. And she wanted this entire fiasco over as soon as possible.

She managed to maintain an air of cool detachment as she helped Jed dish up the stew and put the meal on the table. She sat carefully out of his reach as they ate, greeting his attempts to draw her out with aloof silence. She knew it was the coward's way out, but she was already in over her head, and she wasn't going to deliberately dig herself in any deeper.

The puppies, however, were her downfall. After dinner Jed brought their box into the living room and dumped them out on the floor. Sadie, always the proud mother, sat beaming as Jed sprawled on the carpet to play with her brood.

Erica perched primly on the couch and watched the puppies stumble awkwardly about on wobbly baby legs. After a few moments her resolve slowly melted away. Jed looked so nonthreatening stretched out on his back with a puppy balanced on his stomach that she felt safe in sliding to the floor to cuddle her favorite little black fellow. He squirmed happily in her arms, acting for all the world like he remembered her. Which she knew was ridiculous. No animal that young had a memory. She decided he was just destined to be overly friendly.

An opinion Jed promptly contradicted. Raising himself to one elbow, he smiled across at her. "Boy, he sure likes you. I only get the cold shoulder and fierce baby growls. He treated Mrs. Yosensky the same way when she tried to hold him yesterday."

For some reason Erica felt flattered all out of proportion. As a child, she'd always dreamed of having a dog. For an instant she had the impulse to ask if she could adopt this charming little black waif. She promptly dismissed the idea and set the puppy firmly on the floor with his siblings. She had no room in her life for a pet. She was on the road for Ledbetter Enterprises so much she'd never be home to take care of him.

Jed was watching her, but he said nothing. Instead he fished under an armchair for a bright-red rubber ball which he tossed into the midst of the puppies. With single-minded determination, they waddled after it, stumbling and growling as if in pursuit of some deadly prey. Jed rested his chin on his fists and watched in obvious delight.

Erica noticed that the errant lock of hair had once again tumbled down over his forehead. She longed to reach across and smooth it back. Instead she clasped her hands firmly in her lap and focused on the puppies. Without warning Sadie suddenly waded into the melee, snatched up the ball, and dropped it in Erica's lap.

"She wants you to pay some attention to her," Jed interpreted. "I guess she's jealous. Everyone's always making a fuss over the pups, and she feels left out. I keep forgetting she's not much more than a puppy herself.''

"Okay, Sadie, I'll play with you," Erica laughed as she threw the ball into the kitchen.

With a look of glee, Sadie raced after it and returned in a flash to drop the ball again in Erica's lap. Erica threw the ball several more times, and soon decided Sadie was as stubborn and persistent as her master. To give her arm a rest, she tossed the ball as far as she could down the hallway. Undaunted, Sadie flew after it, returning seconds later with it clasped firmly in her mouth. With a triumphant bark, she launched herself at Erica, landing in her lap with such force that Erica toppled helplessly backwards. Immediately the puppies swarmed in to join their mother in giving Erica a thorough face washing.

Giggling, Erica closed her eyes against the onslaught. Suddenly she sensed, rather than saw, Jed looming over her. She squinted up at him.

"Are you okay?" he asked anxiously.

"Yeah, I'm fine," she sputtered. "Unless they lick me to death."

"All right, you four-footed assailants, back to jail with you." He quickly captured the pups and struggled to his feet with the box. "Come on, Sadie. You're exiled to the back porch until you learn better manners with our guests." He winked at Erica as Sadie fell in behind, looking suitably repentant. "There are some paper towels by the kitchen sink if you want to wash up, Erica."

"Thanks." Erica rose and went into the kitchen, brushing carpet fuzz and dog hair off her expensive skirt. She wet a towel and scrubbed vigorously at her face while Jed shut the dogs away. When she finished, she turned to find him leaning against the counter watching her.

"Sorry I let them get so carried away," he apologized.

"That's all right. No real harm done." Their eyes locked and the familiar electricity arced between them.

He took a step toward her. "You're a very good sport."

She took a step away. "Think nothing of it."

He advanced again. "But I really would like to express my gratitude."

She retreated . . . and felt the wall at her back. "And just how do you propose to do that?"

"Like this." He leaned in deftly and placed an arm on either side of her.

In theory, she knew she could duck under his arms and escape. In reality, she found she couldn't move. She was frozen in place. She watched helplessly through half-closed eyelids as his lips descended on hers; she shivered pleasurably as he stepped in closer and pressed his body against hers. His hands cupped her shoulders, pulling her ever closer until she could feel all the angular planes of him meshing with her own softness. She wanted to resist, but found that she had no power to do so. Her resolve was melting like marshmallows over a raging bonfire.

The warning bell sounded in her brain as never before. Jed was invading her private emotional space, breaching her defenses in a way that threatened the very person she had worked so hard to become. She had never allowed a man such power over her. Her desire to escape the demeaning poverty of her childhood had driven her toward her goal of material success . . . and away from the entanglements that might have hindered her reaching those goals.

And that included men—men who might have brought

her such pleasure as Jed was now bringing. But no. She knew on some primordial level that Jed was unique. Capable of touching some part of her heart... her soul... as no other man ever could.

And she was responding with every fiber of her being—coming alive in a way that she'd never experienced before. On some abstract plane of her mind she had a flash of insight. So this was how it felt to fall in love.

Love!

The word crystalized in her mind, then exploded with a force that set her quivering. *Love!* She couldn't possibly love Jed Daniels. There was no future in it for either of them. A physical attraction to him, she readily acknowledged. But love? No way!

She pushed against him until he released her, then she scrambled to put some distance between them. "I'm sorry," she said breathlessly. "This is my fault. I never should have come here with you tonight."

"What are you talking about? Of course you should've come."

"No. No, I shouldn't have. I had no right to lead you on."

"Lead me on? Erica, *I* kissed *you*."

"But I let you."

Passion smoldered in his eyes. "I doubt you could've stopped me."

Erica hugged herself defensively. "Certainly I could've stopped you. We aren't animals. We're capable of controlling our emotions."

"I don't know about that. My feelings were close to being out of control. And I dare you to deny that you were in any better shape than I was. You excite me, Erica...." Amuse-

Decision of the Heart

ment replaced the passion in his eyes. "And you didn't lead me on."

She bristled. He was laughing at her again. Why should she have expected any different? She'd picked a fine person to fall in love with.

That thought angered her even further. "I see I've amused you once more. I guess we can end the evening on that note. Always leave them laughing—that's my motto!" She whirled to go, tired of trying to deal with a man and a situation she had no chance of ever controlling.

Jed was at her side in two long strides. He caught her arm and forced her to turn to face him. "Erica, I'm sorry I upset you. The thing that amused me was that you thought you were leading me on." Laughter still lurked in his eyes. "It sounded so naive—"

She jerked her arm away. "Go ahead. Laugh. The battle isn't over yet. We'll see who's laughing in the end."

"I am not laughing at you!" he insisted.

"Oh, come on! You haven't taken me seriously since I set foot in this town. You've deliberately maneuvered me into situations where you thought you could make a fool of me. And I'm tired of playing your juvenile games!"

He sobered. "Baby, believe me, my respect for you grows with every encounter. I'm not about to underestimate you. The moment you first walked into my office, I knew I was up against the other team's star player."

"But you still think you can beat me."

"Sure," he admitted. "If I didn't, I might as well give up now. But I will concede that if anyone can give me a run for the money, it's you."

Erica's temper flared. He was still so cocky . . . so confident of triumph. "A run for the money," she mimicked.

"How generous of you. You're so sure of yourself, aren't you? So certain you have all the angles covered."

"Not all the angles. I wasn't counting on this thing between us. Make any rationalization you want. Try as hard as you will to avoid facing up to it. But there's no way you can deny it's real."

Erica shivered at the intensity—and, yes, the truth—of his words. He continued to amaze her. It seemed clear the attraction he professed for her was real. But it was even more clear that he didn't intend to let it interfere with waging an all-out war against the sale.

And neither could she.

She had to win now. It was a point of honor with her on many levels. The foremost being that Jed Daniels needed to be brought down a notch or two. She'd never met anyone so conceited. She was grateful he'd shown her how insensitive he could be. Grateful he'd laughed at her efforts to play fair in the arena of their personal relationship.

Love, ha! How could she have thought for even an instant that she might love him? She'd merely fallen under his spell again. Undeniably, he had a certain magic about him, in his eyes, his touch. . . .

She felt it again as she gathered her things to leave. He made no move to interfere until they reached the car. There he again caught her arm and gently turned her to face him.

The lopsided grin was back in place as he reached up and smoothed her hair. "You can't keep running away like this, Erica. One of these days you'll have to deal with this. But I can wait. There's plenty of time. . . . "

Don't bet on it! she thought to herself. Her time in this wretched place was limited. One week down and counting.

Chapter Seven

The next few days passed in a blur of activity. Mayor Ferris introduced Erica to various businessmen and community leaders, and she pursued each contact with a vengeance—arranging personal briefings for each on Ledbetter Enterprises' plans for Lawn Magic Mowers. Overall, the response was positive, and Erica began to feel cautiously optimistic.

Her evenings were spent writing editorials and speaking to the various clubs. Jed was always there, always flirting. . . . But she managed to sidestep any overt contact. Infuriatingly, that didn't seem to bother him. He seemed content to play some sort of waiting game.

Erica knew she should feel relieved. But she didn't. She only felt numb, as if she were caught in a state of suspended animation. She longed only to return to New York so she could get on with her life.

Hana didn't mention the dinner at Jed's, so Erica decided Mrs. Yosensky must not be as big a gossip as the rest of the town. Erica suspected that if she could just elude Jed for the rest of the week, the rumors would die for good. And so far her luck was holding. . . .

Her luck ran out Tuesday evening, three days before the stockholders' vote on Friday. They were again addressing a group of women, the Business and Professional Women's

Club. Though this group was better educated than the first, Jed still had the same effect on them. As she watched him weave his spell, Erica felt her carefully constructed facade of indifference crumble away. She didn't bother to plot a battle strategy this time. She'd rather admit defeat than linger and watch other women flirt with him. She went through her presentation with robotic perfection, then quickly gathered up her papers to leave.

As she skirted the knot of attractive women clustered around Jed, she felt a familiar stab of rejection—rather like she'd felt when snubbed by the cliquish sororities during her college years. The chic coeds had had no interest in her then, and these women had no interest in her now. It was an appropriate reminder to keep her focused on her mission.

She hurried out to the car parked in front of the Town Hall where the meeting had been held. She placed her briefcase in the backseat and leaned for a moment against the convertible before getting inside. She was more upset than she should be. Certainly more upset than she wanted to be. Since meeting Jed, she'd practically become a basket case—completely at the mercy of her emotions. It was a feeling she didn't enjoy. Blast him!

"You can run, but you can't hide...."

Jed's words from behind her made her breath catch in her throat. She'd celebrated her escape too early. Resignedly, she turned to face him. "Oh, I don't know," she said coolly. "I've managed to carve out a little breathing room for myself these last few days. And the time before the vote is drawing rapidly to a close."

"But this thing between us won't go away at the end of two weeks."

"Perhaps *it* won't. But *I* will. After the vote, I'm history.

Decision of the Heart 95

Maybe you ought to keep your mind on the dwindling number of days left to accomplish your own goal. If, indeed, you sincerely believe the sale will ruin the town."

The teasing glint in his eyes faded to hardness. "Oh, I'm very sincere in that belief, Ms. Stone. And I'm just as sincere in my belief that such a thing won't happen. So you might as well relax and enjoy the social aspects of your stay here."

"I'm not in a social mood, Mr. Daniels. Now, good night."

She deliberately turned her back on him and climbed in the car. She sensed, rather than saw, him leave. Her hands on the steering wheel were shaking, so she reached for her briefcase and pretended to make notes while she composed herself. Gradually her breathing returned to normal. She shut the briefcase and glanced around cautiously. Jed was a few doors down visiting with a shop owner who was out sweeping the sidewalk. Her heart skipped another beat, but determinedly she inserted the key in the ignition.

Then she saw Mary across the street at the Fashion Box, staring in the window at a display of prom dresses. The girl seemed captivated by a frothy pink number with a beaded bodice. Erica knew from her own shopping spree that the store's prices were well beyond anything Mary could afford. Erica felt such empathy for Mary in that moment that she sat unable to move. Again she was a vulnerable teenager, experiencing the bittersweet longing for the beautiful life that hovered cruelly, tantalizingly just beyond her reach—as it did now with Mary.

She and Mary were united . . . in a sisterhood to which the clever young women of the Business and Professional Women's Club could never belong. Not that they would want to. It was a sorority she wished she'd escaped, wished Mary could escape. It warped, punished, brutalized, and left scars no amount of success or carefully cultivated poise could ever completely erase.

And Mary didn't yet have the sophistication of adulthood to hide behind. She was utterly defenseless at this point in her life.

Suddenly a group of adolescent girls emerged from the dress store, arms loaded with purchases. Mary quickly turned away, but not before they'd seen her.

"Picking out your prom dress, Mary?" one taunted.

"Saturday is your dad's payday," another said with a laugh. "Bet he'll rush right over here and buy it for you."

"Who are you kidding?" The third girl sneered. "The only place old Tim Wilson stops on Saturday night is the liquor store, right, Mary?"

Mary pretended not to hear. It was an act of self-preservation Erica herself had practiced often when she'd suffered similar attacks as a child. She knew exactly the humiliation Mary felt as the girl lifted her chin a notch higher and marched stiffly away to disappear around the corner.

Erica could no longer see Mary, but she knew without a doubt what the girl would do next. Mary would break and run, while angry tears coursed down her cheeks. She'd run until she was safely inside whatever miserable shack her father could afford to rent with the money left after his liquor purchases. Then she'd throw herself down on a lumpy bed and cry herself to sleep.

The sisterhood of secret sorrows, Erica thought ironically. Once a member, the dues were extracted for life.

"Erica, are you all right?" Jed's voice at her elbow was

welcome this time. It dragged her from a painful place she hadn't visited in a long while.

As she turned to look at him, she could think of no flippant response. The concern in his eyes deepened and his hand moved to cover hers still clutching the steering wheel. "What's wrong?" he asked kindly.

She somehow forced a false normalcy into her voice. "I guess I was just upset at how those girls treated Mary."

His gaze drifted to the three teenagers making their way lightheartedly down the opposite sidewalk. "Yeah, I saw that. Those thoughtless, spoiled brats deserve a good spanking. Not all the kids in town are like that."

Maybe not all, but the vast majority, she thought. She could testify to that fact from her own unfortunate past.

"I'm sorry that scene disturbed you," Jed continued. "Mary doesn't deserve such treatment."

"No. No, she doesn't," Erica agreed absently.

"Want to come into the drugstore for a malt?" he offered. "There's nothing like ice cream to take a bad taste out of your mouth."

Erica wished such a simplistic remedy would work. However, she knew it wouldn't be that easy to blot the incident out of her mind. Jed didn't understand. But this time it wasn't his fault. He was only trying to help. She smiled in genuine gratitude. "That's very thoughtful, but I don't need the calories. Hana's cooking is really inflating my waistline."

He nodded and stepped away from the car, a troubled frown on his face. "See you tomorrow then."

Without responding, she started the car and pulled away. She turned the corner onto a side street and stopped. She waited until Jed was gone, then she drove back to the dress shop.

Once there, she got out, went inside, and purchased the pink formal.

It was still early when she got back to the rooming house. When she entered she was surprised to see Jed and Allan sitting in the parlor talking. They paused when they saw her. Jed's eyes fell on the dress box, but he said nothing. Both men rose as she stopped in the door.

"Hi, Erica," Allan called. "Jed came by to see you, and I thought I'd keep him company while he waited."

Erica forced a smile. "That was nice of you, Allan. Sorry I was late."

"No problem," Allan responded. "I enjoyed visiting with someone besides Junior for a change. The two of us have been cooped up together for so long, we can practically communicate without speaking."

I know the feeling, Erica almost blurted as her eyes locked with Jed's. Out loud she said only, "How's the paperwork coming, Allan?"

"We're about to wrap it up. I think we can finish with the last few details tomorrow. Which reminds me, I need the car in the morning. I've got to run over to Oklahoma City to the Tax Commission to look up some records. I hope that won't be a problem."

"But we're supposed to speak at some club's pancake breakfast out at the fairgrounds," she protested with a panic-stricken glance at Jed.

"The Kiwanis Club," Jed supplied tersely.

Erica knew Allan was becoming aware of the tension between her and Jed, but he didn't comment on it. "I'm sorry," he said simply. "I'll be back by the middle of the day if that will help."

"Can't you borrow Junior's car?" she asked desperately. "Hana said the fairgrounds are about five miles outside of town."

"Nope. Sorry. Junior's old clunker can barely wheeze around town. You'd think a mechanical genius like Junior would drive a powerful, well-oiled machine, wouldn't you? I can't figure how his mind works."

"I think it only functions in the abstract," Jed put in. "He can plan a project out perfectly on paper, but then he can't seem to get organized enough to put it into production. That's why the company is in so much trouble."

Allan nodded his agreement. "Yeah, that about covers it." He turned to Erica. "Again, I'm sorry about the car."

"I can give you a lift, Erica," Jed offered. "I'll be coming right by here anyway, and we're both going to the same meeting."

To his credit, Erica noticed that Jed hadn't seized upon her misfortune with his usual glee. She sighed and accepted his offer. "Thank you."

"Well, I'll leave you two to discuss . . . whatever," Allan said perceptively. "Good night."

As he left the room, Jed took a step toward her. "I was worried about you. You seemed so upset earlier." His eyes drifted to the dress box again. "But you look better now."

"Yes. Yes I am." She was touched that he'd cared enough to stop by. But right on the heels of that feeling came a surge of annoyance that she'd once more be trapped into being alone with him tomorrow. Oh, well, the pancake breakfast was their last scheduled debate. Then it would all be over except for the last-minute coaxing, cajoling, and reassurances any wavering stockholders might need.

And then she could leave....

"I'm glad you're feeling better." The words Jed spoke to recapture her attention were simple enough. The message in his eyes was infinitely more complex. "I'll see you in the morning. And, remember, dress casually. Everyone at this thing tomorrow will probably have on jeans. I'll be by about eight o'clock."

"I'll be ready." She almost wished he'd take her in his arms, if only for a moment. Somehow she knew his touch would chase the lingering loneliness away. But he only squeezed her arm as he passed, then walked on out the front door without looking back.

The moment he was gone, she understood the reason for his uncharacteristically prudent behavior. Hana was peering through the heavy velvet curtains that separated the parlor from her private sitting room. Erica's agitation increased. She decided not to let the woman get away with such sneakiness. "How are you this evening, Hana?" she called.

Hana didn't appear to be the least embarrassed as she pushed on into the room. "I'm fine, Erica." She made a great show of plumping the pillows on the old horsehair sofa. "I was coming in to straighten up when I saw you had company. I didn't want to interrupt anything between you and Jed."

"There was nothing to interrupt," Erica said crossly.

Hana's knowing smile said clearly that she thought differently. "So, you're riding with him tomorrow to the breakfast, huh?"

"That's right. Allan needs the car to go to Oklahoma City."

Decision of the Heart

"Oh." Hana appeared profoundly disappointed. She eyed the dress box. "More new clothes?"

"This isn't for me. It's a gift for Mary. She's been so good about keeping my room neat."

An affectionate gleam replaced the leer in Hana's eyes. "That's really sweet of you. Mary's probably never had a new dress in her life. I know she'll be grateful."

I hope so, Erica thought to herself. She remembered that having someone notice her poverty as a child had been almost as painful as the poverty itself. "What time will Mary be in in the morning?"

"She's usually here by six to help me start breakfast."

"Could you send her up to my room a little before eight?"

Hana chuckled. "Well, don't dawdle with Mary and keep Jed waiting."

Erica ignored the comment and left the room in disgust. She'd had enough of this town, its people, and the memories it stirred. She couldn't escape fast enough to suit her.

The next morning Erica waited apprehensively as Mary opened the dress box.

For an instant the girl's face lit with yearning, then she closed the box abruptly and pushed it across the bed at Erica. "I don't take charity."

Erica heard all the thinly veiled pain in Mary's voice. "This isn't charity, Mary. It's a gift. In appreciation for all the kindness you've shown me during my stay here. I have a right to say thanks."

It was clear the girl was torn. But it was also clear she wasn't fooled by semantics. "We both know you don't owe me anything for the things I've done for you. I was just doing my job. You bought this because you feel sorry for me. I saw you watching last night at the dress shop."

Erica knew then she'd have to take a personal risk to get through to Mary. "It's true I felt sorry for you last night. But only because I was reminded of things that happened to me long ago. I've been where you are."

An array of emotions flickered across Mary's face. "I thought you seemed different from most people. So your old man was a drunk, too?"

Erica nodded. "Yes. My father was an alcoholic."

Mary sighed, and her tone softened somewhat. "I'm sorry. I didn't mean to sound so disrespectful of my father. It's just hard to live like this sometimes...." She pulled the box toward her and opened the lid again. "He really cares for me. I can see it on his face when he's sober. And he's sorry for how bad things have become. It's just that he can't handle the pain."

Erica was close to tears. "Your father sounds a lot like mine."

Mary stared deeply into Erica's eyes. "Did your mother die, too?"

"No, she ran off with another man—my father's best friend. We heard a few years later that they'd both been killed in a car wreck." Erica shivered as she remembered the morning they'd gotten the news. Her father's binge had lasted for a week that time.

"Wow! No wonder your dad drank."

"Yeah. I felt really sorry for him. The shame of it all. . . . We lived in a small town, and the news of my mother's infidelity spread quickly."

"Did the kids in your school know?"

"Oh, yes. Apparently their parents talked openly in front of them."

"Don't you just hate that—the gossip, I mean? I can't wait until I'm old enough to leave this place and go somewhere where no one knows me."

"Your education's the answer."

"I already figured that out. After I graduate next year I have a full scholarship to the University of Oklahoma. My teachers pulled all kinds of strings to help me get it." Mary laughed cynically. "I guess they feel sorry for me, too."

"Their string-pulling wouldn't have done any good if you hadn't made the grades. Just be grateful for their help, whatever their motivation. I would never have made it out of my hometown if my teachers hadn't helped me."

"But you did make it—and made it big. Now you live in New York and have a glamorous career. Maybe I will, too. Someday. . . . You know, you're the only person I've ever met who's had it as tough as I have. And you beat the odds. That gives me hope."

"Dear, you should have all the hope in the world. You're just beginning in life. And you're one step ahead of me when I was your age." Erica indicated the dress. "At least you're taking a little time out to have a good time. Who's your date for the prom?"

The girl's face fell. "I don't have one. None of the creepy boys in this town would risk their precious reputations by going out with the daughter of the town drunk. But Mrs. Riley, the prom sponsor, asked me to come and help her serve at the refreshment table. At first I said no, because I didn't have anything to wear. But now. . . . " Mary caressed the pretty beaded fabric, then looked across at Erica and winked. "Now at least on prom night the boys will get a good look at what they're missing."

Erica laughed with Mary, but it took an effort considering the lump in her throat. How much she'd longed for just such a chance to show off on prom night. Only her chance had never come.

Mary carefully closed the box with tears glistening in her eyes. "Thanks for the dress. It's the nicest thing anyone's ever done for me."

Tears filled Erica's eyes as well. "You're welcome. But you realize I didn't do it just for you. I also did it for me."

Mary nodded, and Erica knew that somehow the girl did indeed understand. Mary smiled in a way that made her look far older than fifteen—and far wiser. "Don't worry about me after you leave. You made it. I will, too." She hugged the dress box to her. "Good-bye."

"Good-bye." Erica stood staring at the door long after Mary was gone. She was glad she'd bought the dress. In easing a bit of Mary's pain, she'd managed to reach back into her past and erase some of her own.

She closed her eyes and said a silent prayer for Mary. The girl had so much struggle ahead of her. But Erica knew that in the end Mary would come out all the stronger for it, as she herself had done.

She did her best to shake off the pervading air of sadness and refocus on the day ahead. The last debate. A milestone. The finish line lay in view, and she and Jed were neck and neck sprinting toward the wire.

She couldn't let the emotional experience with Mary become a stumbling block in the race before her. It was almost eight. Time to meet Jed downstairs. She checked her appearance in the mirror one last time. She'd opted for tailored slacks and comfortable loafers over jeans and sneakers. Since she was speaking, she felt she should be a bit more dressed up than the crowd. She looked perfect—poised and glamorous. No trace remained of the insecure, haunted child she had been. Mary would reach this point someday. She just knew it. She grabbed her purse and headed out the door.

Chapter Eight

A solid round of applause broke out as Erica concluded her speech and left the podium. Jed gave her a cocky wink as he stepped up to take her place. The audience had been warm and responsive to her. Clearly he expected a similar reception.

She watched him with a curious objectivity as he began his spiel. By now she almost had it memorized—as he surely did hers. Disjointedly, it occurred to her that the jeans and formfitting Western shirt showed off his broad shoulders and trim waist even better than a suit.

She shivered involuntarily as she realized she knew just how far her arms would reach around that waist and how it felt to rest her head in the curve of that shoulder.... She gave herself a mental shake and surfaced from her daydream. She then did her best to pay attention. But she was nevertheless grateful when Jed's time was up and he once more took his seat beside her. It wasn't so easy to stare at him there.

The moderator's call for questions was greeted by silence. The group seemed satisfied with the information they'd received through the speeches. More and more these last few days, that had been the case. Apparently most of the stockholders had already made up their minds, which was as it should be at this point. The vote was only two days away.

Decision of the Heart

For a moment it seemed the session might end without a single question. Then a burly, middle-aged man rose at the back of the auditorium.

The moderator gave him the floor. "The chair recognizes Zach Ramsey of Ramsey Construction."

Ramsey cleared his throat. "Yeah, Jed, what I'd like to know is why you're fighting this buyout so hard."

Jed seemed startled by the question. "I thought I'd made that clear over the past few weeks. I feel selling the plant to outsiders endangers the town's economy—"

Ramsey interrupted. "No, I mean what's your reason on a personal level?"

Jed's surprise increased. "Why, I have none. I'm not a stockholder. I have nothing to gain one way or the other."

"And nothing to lose," Ramsey continued. "That bothers a bunch of us, Jed. If you stood to lose something yourself, we might be more inclined to listen to you. As it is, seems like you're asking us to make a mighty big sacrifice. We'd be giving up thousands of dollars—money that would mean a lot to our families." A murmur of support for Ramsey's statement ran through the crowd.

"Well, now, Zach," Jed replied, "you're not hurting all that much financially, what with all those new houses you're building."

Erica knew Jed was trying to lighten the mood by joking with Ramsey. But she also sensed this was the wrong approach to take with this crowd. They were obviously not in a joking mood.

And neither was Ramsey. "It's true I'm doing okay with my business," he replied angrily, "but a lot of these folks ain't so lucky. You gonna make light of their problems, too?" The audience again murmured agreement.

Jed held up his hand for silence. "I apologize. I didn't intend to sound insensitive to anyone's problems. I simply think we need to keep the big picture in mind. True, selling the plant will mean an immediate short-term gain for the stockholders. But what about the long-term cost? If the plant closes, the whole town will go under."

"We can all see the danger if that should take place," Ramsey broke in. "But Miss Stone's about convinced us it ain't gonna happen. So, could be we'd end up needlessly throwing away good money if we let you scare us outa this deal. Especially since you ain't got nothing to lose yourself."

Erica felt a surge of triumph. Judging from their expressions, the crowd overwhelmingly agreed with Ramsey. Over the last few days, she'd sensed a growing acceptance of her position. But this was the first concrete evidence she'd had to verify she'd finally won. She should never have doubted. As B.J. always said, money will out.

It appeared to be a rude awakening for Jed, however. He wore a stunned scowl as he surveyed the crowd. Erica avoided his gaze. He almost deserved to lose because of his cocky attitude alone. But still, he'd waged the war for wholly altruistic purposes. And defeat was always harder to bear when one viewed the fight as a battle between good and evil. She almost felt sorry for him. Almost—but not quite. The taste of victory was too sweet.

The meeting broke up quickly, and no one lingered to visit. It was just as well. Jed seemed in no mood to socialize. He made no effort to talk as they began the short drive back to town. So Erica sat silently with her eyes firmly fixed on the lush countryside gliding past outside the car window. Strangely she had no desire to rub it in.

Jed suddenly broke the silence. "Does your interest in the Victorian era extend to houses?" he asked in a surprisingly cheerful tone.

Erica glanced over at him suspiciously. "Of course. I love those old houses. Outwardly they appear so whimsical, with all that gingerbread trim. But structurally, they're solid as a rock—built to survive for hundreds of years. You can't beat a combination like that."

"Then I want you to see my family's old homestead." He swung the car off the highway onto a dirt road that veered away to the right. "It's been handed down for five generations now. My great-great-grandfather staked a claim to it in the Land Run of 1889. It belongs to me now."

Erica studied him through squinted eyes. Now they were off on a jolly sight-seeing tour. She could only conclude that he wasn't as crushed by his defeat as she had at first imagined. It frustrated her that she could never quite figure him out. She turned again to stare out the window.

They were passing a neat-looking farmhouse set close to the road. An elderly man in overalls was out in the yard tinkering with an old pickup. Jed raised his hand in greeting. "That's Bud Landry. His land borders mine. He keeps an eye on the old place for me."

"So your homestead is nearby?"

"Yep, right at the top of this hill." A few yards past the Landry house, Jed turned into a narrow driveway that meandered lazily up a wooded hillside. Apparently it was seldom traveled, for encroaching underbrush slapped at the sides of the car. The atmosphere wasn't depressing, however. Instead, Erica felt an air of peaceful seclusion as sunlight spilled through the overhanging branches to dapple the road.

Then abruptly the trees gave way to a small clearing.

Gnarled blackjack oaks surrounded it on three sides, while on the fourth the ground dropped away dramatically to a hay meadow in the valley below. And right in the center of the clearing sat one of the most beautiful two-story Victorian farmhouses Erica had ever seen. It was painted a pristine white and had leaded glass windows throughout and a round tower on the corner.

"Oh, Jed, it's gorgeous!" she exclaimed as he stopped the car.

"Yeah, I've always thought so. I spent many happy hours here before my grandmother died and my grandfather closed the place and moved into town."

"But why on earth would he want to move from here?"

"I don't think he really wanted to. It's just that he was getting on in years, and his eyesight was failing. By living in town, he eliminated the long five-mile drive back and forth to work each day."

Erica laughed. "That's so funny. You act like a five-mile drive is a big deal. Why, people in New York think nothing of commuting ten times that far just to live in a place like this."

"Is that what you plan to do someday?"

Erica stiffened. "No, it's not for me. I'd feel like life was passing me by if I were stuck way out in the sticks somewhere."

"Yeah, all of us poor stick dwellers are certainly to be pitied by you who have the good life."

She didn't miss the sarcasm in his voice. It reminded her of the basic conflict between them. There was no point in getting into it again. "To each his own," she said simply.

"Yeah, I suppose." The sarcasm was gone. Apparently

Decision of the Heart

he'd decided, as she had, to let the matter drop. "Want to look around?" he offered.

"Can we?"

"Sure. The place has been vacant for the past ten years."

"Ten years! But it looks so well cared for."

"Well, Bud Landry has the farmland leased. And under the conditions of the lease, he has to maintain the house—keep a sound roof on it, keep the exterior painted, things like that. He's been good about it, too. Most of my hundred and sixty acres is rich river bottom land, and he doesn't want to lose it. He turns a hefty profit on it every year."

Erica followed him across the overgrown lawn, marveling at the rosebushes and hardy perennials that battled the weeds for dominance in what obviously had once been a meticulously tended garden. Without thinking, she bent to pull an ugly thistle and toss it aside. She blushed as she looked up and found Jed watching her.

"So you like flowers, too, huh?" He smiled. "They were my grandmother's passion, as you can probably tell."

Erica didn't respond. She paused on the porch to gaze down on the hay meadow as Jed unlocked the door. "Your ancestors certainly built the house to take advantage of the scenery," she said softly.

Jed appeared pleased with her praise. "Yeah. Sometimes early in the morning, you can see deer grazing down there. And all sorts of wildlife live in the woods out back—rabbits, raccoons, squirrels, you name it." He pushed open the door and stood aside. "After you."

The house was as charming inside as it was out. The floor plan was fairly standard for the era, with front and back parlors on one side of the wide entry hall and a library and dining room on the other. At the back a huge, old-fashioned country kitchen ran the width of the house. There were, however, special touches that set it apart from its contemporaries. Each room had a wood-burning fireplace, there were hardwood floors throughout, and the burnished oak woodwork gleamed unblemished even through the dust.

Erica finally turned to Jed with a puzzled grin. "Living in this beautiful old place would be paradise. I wish I had it in New York. Why don't you move out here yourself?"

"Oh, I plan to someday. Presently, it's just not practical."

"Not practical? Why?"

"Because of the very features you've been oohing and ahing over—the large rooms with the high ceilings and the wood-burning fireplaces. This old monstrosity is impossible to heat and cool. There's no insulation in the walls, no central heat and air-conditioning, the plumbing's outdated, and there's only one tiny bathroom at the end of the upstairs hallway. The bath was added as an afterthought around 1920. It's barely functional now."

"But all that can be fixed. There are companies that specialize in updating historic homes without compromising the integrity."

"And those companies charge huge fees. Fees I can't afford right now—and probably not in the foreseeable future. The paper is just now showing a profit again after being on the slide for the last decade."

"Well, maybe remodeling wouldn't be all that expensive. Show me the bedrooms. I'll bet it would be simple to add a couple of more baths."

Jed shrugged and led the way up the sweeping staircase to the second floor. The bathroom he'd mentioned was at the top of the stairs and was indeed small, dark, and outdated. However, the four bedrooms were just as Erica had imagined—absolutely huge, with oversized windows that looked out into the woods.

She made a quick tour and finally stopped in the bedroom across from the master suite. "See? All these rooms have to be at least twenty by twenty. You could take four feet off the end of this one and the one next door. That would give you a strip eight by twenty. You could use half that strip for back-to-back walk-in closets—one opening into each bedroom. Then the other half could be converted to an eight-by-ten bathroom accessible from both bedrooms. That would be a perfect setup for children...."

Her voice trailed off as she realized the children in question would be Jed's. And what of their mother—who would that be? An ugly surge of jealousy swept over her. She glanced up and found Jed watching her again. Did the twinkle in his eye mean that he'd guessed her thoughts? She scowled at him, hoping to wipe the smug grin off his face.

It didn't work. The grin broadened. "Go on," he prompted. "What do you suggest for the other rooms ... particularly the master bedroom?"

Erica's heart thudded erratically. Maybe it wasn't such a good idea to discuss bedrooms with a man she found so attractive. But she couldn't stop now or he'd know for sure where her thoughts were straying. She dodged around him and hurried to the doorway of the master bedroom.

The extra space provided by the second-floor section of the corner tower would make a great sitting room, she decided. It had windows on all sides—the perfect place to laze in a rocking chair and enjoy the sunrise while the kids and a loving husband ... *Jed* ... were still asleep.

Predictably he came up to stand behind her. She moved

on into the room to escape him and stood with her back to the wall. "It would be a shame to lose any of the space in this room," she plunged ahead. "I'd take the full eight feet off the fourth bedroom next door. Again, half the space could be used for an eight-by-ten walk-in closet for this room which... er... both the husband and wife would share. Then the other section could be a private master bath. That would leave the fourth bedroom twelve by twenty, still plenty large enough for a guest room. And anytime it was occupied, the guests could use the small bathroom at the end of the hall."

"Perfect!" Jed leaned nonchalantly against the door frame so that their shoulders were almost touching. "Now all I have to do is strike it rich so I can afford to do all this remodeling."

Erica wanted to cheerfully reassure him he'd have the money in no time, but she knew that would be a lie. In a place like Willow Springs, Jed's earning capacity was limited. He surely knew that, too. She'd been thoughtless to pursue this conversation about restoring the house. It had only turned into an awkward situation for both of them.

Still, Jed seemed unwilling to drop the matter. "Okay, Ms. Antique Expert," he challenged playfully, "what type of furniture do you envision in here? For instance, the bed...."

Her heart lurched at the provocative scene his words brought to mind. He was playing games again, trying to turn this into another arena of combat. He probably thought she didn't have the nerve to accept this latest challenge. Well, she wasn't about to let him know he was getting to her.

Nerve, she had. It was good sense she was lacking.

Decision of the Heart

She plunged ahead, realizing full well she was walking willingly into a trap. "Probably a big mahogany four-poster. And a big heavy dresser for...ah...your wife, and a gentleman's armoire against this wall for you."

Jed met her gaze, then nodded toward the tower area. "And a sitting room over there with a rocking chair."

"Yes, a rocking chair...." Erica said breathlessly. She'd felt before that Jed could read her mind, but never so much as in this moment. The image of herself with him in this room in such a bed as she'd described was so real it was frightening. She felt like a helpless medieval princess caught in a spell. She had to escape those hypnotic blue eyes....

She bolted across to the tower and stood looking out over the countryside. "The view is great from here." She laughed shakily. "Perfect for watching—"

"—the sunset?" Jed interrupted as he came up behind her.

"Or the sunrise," she said irritably. She stiffened as he stepped in closer and slid his arms around her waist. He seemed satisfied just to hold her, so she closed her eyes and gradually relaxed against him.

The contentment she felt in his arms was bittersweet, tinged with the longing for things that could never be. Yet that didn't dull the pleasurable sensations that coursed through her body as Jed slowly bent his head and began nibbling the side of her neck.

"Yahoo, anybody home?"

Erica tensed as the disembodied voice floated up from the downstairs foyer. "Who is that?" she demanded in a hoarse whisper.

Jed laughed and released her. "It sounds like Bud Landry. Come on. I'll introduce you."

The weathered little man at the bottom of the stairs watched Erica with a suggestive leer as they descended. "Howdy, Jed," he said with mock civility, all the while keeping his eyes on her. "Thought I'd come over and see if you was satisfied with how I'm keepin' up the house."

Jed glanced at Erica. She did nothing to hide her disgust with the farmer's open ogling. Jed quickly stepped between them, forcing Landry to look at him. "The house appears in fine shape, Bud," he said cheerfully. "I have no complaints."

Landry nodded. "Good, good. Lucky I ain't been neglecting my duties, since you started bringin' yer dates out here." His eyes shifted to Erica again. "It is a good private place for gettin' better acquainted...."

Erica's mood darkened at the inference the man was making. She returned his mocking gaze unflinchingly.

Again Jed stepped between them. "Miss Stone collects antique furniture, Bud, from the same era as this house. I thought she'd enjoy seeing a setting in which her pieces might have been used."

Landry chuckled. "Does she own one of them big old-fashioned beds? I noticed you showed her the bedrooms right off."

The last comment even offended Jed. He gave Landry a warning glower.

The man's leer disappeared promptly, and he cleared his throat. "Well, Jed, it's about time to renew the lease. You open to the same terms?"

"I might be." Jed draped an arm around the old man's

Decision of the Heart 117

shoulders. "I'll walk out with you, and we'll set a time to discuss it."

Landry didn't resist as Jed ushered him out of the house. Erica waited in the porch swing while the two of them went on to the pickup. She noticed absently that a gray mass of clouds had boiled up on the horizon and was moving in at a rapid pace. So much for a bright, tranquil summer afternoon. But it was just as well. The new grayness better matched her darkening mood.

Landry's insulting remarks echoed in her mind. The man had some nerve!

And there stood Jed, leaning against the battered pickup, chatting pleasantly as though nothing had happened. She was almost as mad at him as she was at Landry. Finally the old man started the engine, and Jed gave a cordial wave as the pickup disappeared down the driveway.

Jed was still grinning when he returned to the house and plopped down on the porch steps. He reached out to give the swing a playful shove. "I see someone here is no longer a happy camper."

Trust him to make a joke out of this. Well, to her it was no laughing matter. She glowered down at him.

He chuckled. "Hey, I'm not to blame for Bud's wisecrack about the bedrooms. You got us into that one. *You* wanted to see the upstairs."

It infuriated Erica to admit he was right. But still she saw no humor in what had happened. She stared back at him coldly.

"Oh, all right," he persisted good-naturedly. "Since you apparently aren't willing to laugh this off, I'll just have to come up with some other reason to put that lovely smile back on your face." His bravado slipped a little and an edge of weary resignation slid into his voice. "How about if I throw in the towel and declare you winner of our fabled debates? The tide's turned in your favor. Barring divine intervention, the sale of the lawn mower plant will be approved."

Erica still couldn't quite accept that he was being so magnanimous in defeat. "And what brought about this sudden surrender?"

"I suppose that exchange with Zach Ramsey today forced me to be honest with myself. Most of the townspeople have lived all their lives on the brink of poverty. They see this sale as their one chance to strike it rich. I guess I didn't fully realize that when I launched my opposition. I still think they'll be giving up long-term security for short-term financial gain. The money from the sale will be spent in no time and will have no lasting effect on the town's economy. But I've done my best to point that out to them to no avail. So, cheer up. You've won."

He was right, Erica acknowledged grudgingly. And she'd been on the verge of allowing her anger with Bud Landry to rob her of the thrill of victory. She needed to get this whole incident back in perspective. She'd accomplished her goal. In the long run, that's all that mattered. Putting up with a dirty-minded old farmer was only a temporary aggravation, one that would fade quickly in significance once she left Willow Springs behind. Which couldn't be too soon for her—despite the fact that the town held *one* obvious attraction for her.

A sidelong glance at Jed brought on another wave of bittersweet longing.

"Aren't you going to congratulate me for being a good loser?" he prodded.

"Congratulations," she said blandly. "But I hope you'll understand if I check this towel you're throwing in for hidden weapons."

He only chuckled again.

Her suspicions increased. He had to be up to something. She suddenly felt that, on some obscure level, Jed wasn't admitting defeat at all. That fact seemed to be borne out by the spark of challenge glinting in his eyes. Clearly the game-playing wasn't over yet.

And she was bound and determined to remain in the competition until the final bell sounded . . . even though the most grueling rounds might yet lie ahead.

Chapter Nine

Jed stood abruptly and pulled her to her feet. "I think we need to get on back to town. I don't like the looks of that storm that's coming in."

Erica agreed that the cloud bank looked decidedly more menacing than it had only a few minutes earlier. "I suppose we're in for some rain."

"I hope rain's all we get," he said tersely. "I've never personally seen a tornado cloud, only pictures on television. But that sure looks like it could be one." As if to confirm his prediction, a blast of hot air hit with enough force to send Erica reeling backward a step. He reached out a hand to steady her, then urged her on ahead of him toward the car. "Come on! There's no time to waste."

It took about five minutes to reach the blacktop road into town, and by then the leading edge of the storm was directly above them. Erica could see the drooping pockets of wind-heavy clouds sagging and swirling overhead.

Then suddenly one of the drooping appendages trailed lazily to the ground and began rotating madly, sucking up loose dirt and debris from the plowed field to the left of the highway. A solid wall of whirling wind several yards wide was heading straight toward them—a classic tornado if ever there was one. Already Erica could feel the suction battering the car.

Decision of the Heart

Terror gripped her heart. They could easily be killed if the storm overtook them. "Oh, Jed, what are we going to do?" she cried.

"Well, for sure we can't outrun it!" he yelled above the deafening noise. "We'd better take cover under that bridge up ahead. When I stop the car, get out and slide down the embankment as fast as you can. I'll be right behind."

Though it was a struggle, Jed somehow managed to keep the car on the road the short distance to the bridge. As it stopped, Erica felt it begin to rock with the force of the wind. She fought to push the door open as Jed slid toward her across the seat. He reached around to help, then put an arm around her as they scrambled down the embankment. Once inside the round concrete culvert under the roadway, they huddled together, arms about each other, heads down.

The wind was at gale force now, buffeting them with stinging pellets of dirt and dried vegetation. The storm roared by only inches above their heads, sounding for all the world like a speeding freight train. The ground vibrated with frightening intensity, and Erica feared the whole culvert would crack and fall in on top of them.

They heard the unmistakable sound of rending metal, and Erica glanced out to see Jed's car go spinning past the end of the culvert. It revolved with the funnel a couple of full turns, then crashed to the ground in the wheat field to the right of the road. The tornado continued its dizzying dance across the field, and she watched transfixed as a small wooden barn in its path exploded and was sucked up into the whirling vortex.

Then, as suddenly as it had descended, the funnel lifted to the sagging underbelly of the main cloud. Outside, an eerie silence settled over the ravaged countryside. Erica held her breath, unable to believe it could end so abruptly.

With a ragged sigh, Jed loosened his hold on her. "Thank goodness!" he breathed. "For a while, I thought this whole bridge was going to be sucked apart like that barn."

"Yeah, me, too." Erica felt almost giddy with relief. The danger was apparently over, but still she was reluctant to leave the circle of Jed's arms. And glancing up into those incredible blue eyes, she thought she read a similar reluctance on his part to let her go.

"Guess we'd better get out of here," he muttered as he released her. He led the way out of the culvert, and Erica scrambled after him.

The scene that greeted them had a bizarre, surrealistic quality. In front of them, the black wall of cloud writhed and swirled ominously. Behind them, the sun slanted in under the rear edge of the cloud bank, bathing the tornado's path of destruction in a cheerful golden glow. Around them, a warm gentle rain began to fall.

Erica stared in dismay. How could any scene be so beautiful and so fraught with destruction at the same time?

Wordlessly, Jed left her to jog across the wheat field to his car. Outwardly, the vehicle appeared unscathed, and she watched him climb in and try the ignition. Only silence rewarded his effort.

"Internal damage," he reported as he loped back to her. "Being picked up and dropped back to earth didn't do the old girl any good. You game for a brisk walk into town? It's only a couple of miles. We can make it in half an hour." Jed's eyes were fixed on the storm in front of them. "That wall cloud has more than one funnel in it, and it's headed right toward the center of town. I want to be on hand to help after that thing blows through."

He'd barely finished speaking when another fingerlike vortex snaked toward the ground. A distant farm building in its path was sucked apart and swirled up in the air in chunks. Apparently the ordeal wasn't over yet.

The shiver that shook Erica's body was brought on by more than the chill of the rain. When Jed caught her hand and led her out, she didn't resist. She felt as much of a responsibility to help as he did.

The pace Jed set was brisk, and as her body warmed to the exercise, Erica was glad for the feel of the cool rain on her flushed skin.

The tornado damage became more pronounced as they neared town. With incredible whimsy the funnel had hopscotched across the countryside, wreaking havoc in no particular pattern. Two houses stood side by side along a sparsely populated side street. One was demolished while the other stood untouched. Cars were plucked seemingly at random from among those parked in the streets to be overturned or upended against light poles. A befuddled chicken perched dazedly high above the ground where it had been deposited on an electrical line, too afraid to risk a flight to earth.

Then, oddly, the damage ceased. The downtown section appeared to have come through the storm unharmed. A broad smile of relief spread across Jed's face as the *Gazette* office came into view. "It's a miracle," he breathed. "Not even a broken window that I can see."

The throng of onlookers clogging the sidewalks seemed as amazed as Jed. They milled about, murmuring similar statements of disbelief. Jed grabbed Erica's hand and forced his way through the crowd toward the newspaper.

At they stepped into the building, Erica got the strange sensation of having entered a beehive. The *Gazette* staff was scurrying about at a frantic pace. It was a moment before anyone even noticed she and Jed had come in.

Lucille finally looked up from her typewriter and saw them. "Hey, boss, you made it back!" she exclaimed. "What a relief . . . even though you two look like a couple of drowned rats. Where were you when the storm hit?"

"On the way back to town." Jed ran his fingers through his wet hair. "We had to take cover in a culvert. We'd no sooner gotten out of the station wagon when the tornado took it for a little spin. It's now disabled in Bill Whitson's wheat field. We had to walk the rest of the way in the rain. What about here in town—anybody hurt or killed?"

"Nope. Everyone's safe and accounted for, as far as we can tell from the police reports. The tornado sirens went off right on cue, and everybody got to storm shelters in time. All of us huddled down in the basement till the all clear sounded. Even the property damage isn't all that serious. A few overturned cars and some broken tree limbs. Seems the storm stayed on the ground right up to the west edge of town, then lifted as it went over. George is out now seeing if it set down again out to the east. He should be back anytime with a full report."

"Good!" Jed looked relieved. "Where are we with today's edition?"

"The presses are ready to roll. Madge and I went ahead with the layout, just in case you didn't make it back in time. We knew you'd want to devote the front page to coverage of the tornado, so at the top we put a three column photo

Decision of the Heart

of the funnel on the ground, along with a story of the damage. Then we devoted the bottom half of the page to a collage of smaller pictures with captions. Pete got some great shots. In fact, he stayed out so long photographing the blamed thing, he just barely made it into the basement before it hit. He has the film developed already, and while it's drying, he dashed back out to take more pictures of the aftermath. You're welcome to see the layout and make any changes you want.''

"I'm sure it will be fine," Jed affirmed. "Sounds like just what I would've done if I'd been here. I'm proud of all of you."

Jed's praise prompted a sea of smiles, though Erica noticed no one even paused in their work. Apparently Jed's efforts to develop initiative among his employees had been more successful than he'd thought. This crisis had merely provided the first real opportunity for them to act on their own. She remembered how sure she'd been on the flight out that Jed wouldn't dare delegate responsibility. Even when he'd spoken of his efforts earlier, she hadn't quite believed him. Obviously, she'd been wrong about him again.

The phone rang then, and Jed grabbed it. After a few terse sentences, he hung up. "That was the *Daily Oklahoman* in Oklahoma City. They want us to fax them some photos as soon as possible for tonight's edition. How's that, people? The big boys want to play with us!"

A cheer went up! The staff of the *Gazette* was truly in its element now—operating as an admittedly outdated, but still functional, well-oiled machine.

Pete rushed through the door at that moment, waving an exposed roll of film. "I got some fantastic human-interest stuff here! The electric company crew went out looking for line damage after the storm and couldn't find any. But they got all caught up in rescuing this pitiful old chicken marooned way up on one of their wires. They shut off the electricity and went up in the cherry picker to grab the chicken. Crazy as it sounds, I'll swear that old hen had a grateful look on her face—and I captured it all with my trusty telephoto lens. The readers will eat it up!''

Another cheer went up, and Erica found herself smiling in relief. The crisis must truly be over, she reasoned, if the most pressing rescue to be mounted was that of the chicken.

Jed clapped Pete on the back. "Nice work, Pete, my man. I have more good news. The *Daily Oklahoman* wants to use three or four of your best shots. I said yes, providing they gave our paper *and you* a byline. Send the same photos out over the wire service when you get them printed. There's no telling how many papers will run them here in the state and maybe even nationwide."

"That's great!" Pete exclaimed. "At last—national recognition! My career is officially launched. *Time* magazine, here I come!"

"Don't you think you should worry about graduating from high school first?" Lucille spoke up wryly.

"Hey, today—the wire service. Tomorrow—advanced algebra. There's nothing I can't accomplish. Guess I'd better go see if the film is dry.''

Erica stood in the middle of the floor, watching the easy interaction among the newspaper staff and feeling like an outsider. Her bedraggled appearance did nothing to bolster her confidence. Her wet clothes clung to her like a clammy shroud and her hair was plastered to her head. She longed to get back to the boardinghouse and change.

Decision of the Heart

As if reading her thoughts, Jed gave a burst of final instructions, then strode over to her. "Thanks for being so patient while I got things lined up. Come on. I'll walk you over to Hana's so you can get cleaned up."

"Nonsense. Your place is here. I don't need an escort. I can make it six blocks on my own."

"Hey, everything's well in hand. You've just witnessed that. Besides, I need to get out and assess the damage. It will help me know which stories to run in tomorrow's paper. Now, don't waste time arguing."

Before Erica could protest further, George shuffled through the door clad in a bright-yellow slicker and drooping rain hat.

"Boy, is this town lucky," the old man cried as he shrugged arthritically out of his rain gear. "That tornado took one giant step over the center of town and came down again on the other side. It only tore up one little old house on the west edge and a couple of the older homes down at the east end by the park—" He broke off as his nearsighted gaze fell on Jed. "Boss! I didn't see you there when I first came in."

A strained hush had fallen at George's news. Now Erica waited breathlessly with the others for Jed to ask the next logical question.

He grew visibly tense. "Did it get my house?"

George nodded. "Yeah. Tore it up pretty bad. I would've been more tactful about telling you, but I honestly didn't think I'd be the one to break the news. I thought you'd go straight home once you hit town."

Before Jed could respond, Hana burst through the door. She smiled in relief as she spied them. "Erica! Jed! Land sakes, I was worried sick about you. Came over to see if anyone here had heard from you. You two okay?"

"We're fine," Erica assured her. "How's everything at your place?"

"Wind ripped off a few shingles is all." She paused and looked pointedly at Jed. "Houses down by the park was the hardest hit."

Jed sighed. "Yeah, we heard. Well, it's not like I had a house full of valuables. What furniture I owned can readily be replaced at any secondhand shop. There's nothing I'm really attached to except. . . . "

Erica's mind had traveled through the same thought process as his. She finished the sentence when he couldn't. "Except Sadie and the pups."

Hana's eyes widened. "Oh, them poor little dogs! Come on. I've got my car outside. I'll drive you over."

Outside, the rain had finally stopped. As they drove through town, Erica saw that cleanup efforts were well under way. Already much of the debris in the streets had been cleared away. She was impressed and touched as they passed scene after scene of neighbor helping neighbor. Everywhere trucks and trailers were being loaded with broken tree limbs and uprooted shrubbery. Even small children were enthusiastically raking yards and sweeping driveways. At the rate the townspeople were moving, it wouldn't take long for things to return to normal.

When they reached the park, however, the scene grew more bleak. The roof was blown off the bandstand and several large trees lay toppled and broken. A police barricade blocked the street, and an officer was turning casual traffic away. Jed had Hana drop them off at the corner, and they continued on foot.

Erica's heart plummeted when Jed's house came in sight. The back half of the roof had been lifted neatly off and deposited on the ground. The rear wall of the house and the screened-in porch had been shoved in as if by a giant hand. It now rested at a forty-five-degree angle against an interior wall.

But even so, Jed's house had fared better than Mrs. Yosensky's. Hers lay in a crumpled heap with only the chimney standing upright. She and a group of relatives were digging through the rubble trying to salvage a few possessions.

Jed walked over to her. "I'm sorry," he said simply. "I can lend a hand as soon as I check on my dogs."

"Oh, Jed, I've got more help than I need really," the old woman said with cheerful stoicism. "See to your own place."

Jed nodded. "Well, let me know if there's anything I can do."

"I will. Same goes for you. Now, shoo. We both got things to do."

Jed smiled and gave her a parting hug before leading the way around the house. Erica followed along wordlessly, awed by the scene she'd just witnessed. How could two people who'd suffered such loss behave so calmly?

Beside the collapsed wall, Jed got down on his knees and began to call. "Sadie! Sadie, here girl!" He was rewarded by a volley of happy barks. He looked relieved. "Well, at least she's alive. Now the problem is getting her out." He grabbed a large piece of lumber and tossed it aside.

"Shouldn't we wait for help?" Erica asked.

"I'd be embarrassed to ask." Jed nodded pointedly toward Mrs. Yosensky's house. "There are people who need assistance more than I do."

Erica knew he was right. She pushed up her sleeves. "Then let's get busy."

"You're kidding, right?"

She grinned. "Do I look like I'm kidding? Now, grab one end of this timber. Together I think we can move it."

Jed's astonishment gave way to a look of gratitude. Between them, they were able to wrestle the fallen beam out into the backyard. With much tedious, backbreaking effort they managed to clear a tunnel of sorts behind the collapsed wall angling toward the corner where Sadie's box had been. At one point, Erica was certain she heard a determined scratching coming from inside the wreckage and envisioned Sadie trying to dig her way out.

Which apparently was the case. For when they moved aside a splintered piece of kitchen cabinet, a bright-eyed Sadie squirmed through to freedom. The dog licked Jed's face frantically, then bounded into Erica's lap.

Erica caught her up and hugged her. "You poor darling! We're glad to see you, too. I wish your babies could come to us like you did."

Jed gave a tired sigh and fixed Sadie with a mock glower. "Lassie would go back in there and carry her puppies to safety one at a time, you know."

"In the movies," Erica emphasized with a weary grin. "Unfortunately, this is the real world."

"Unfortunately." He reached in and jerked out a piece of wallboard, causing the material wedged in around it to fall in a shower of dust.

Erica feared for a moment that their access would be blocked completely. But when the dust cleared, a narrow passageway had opened up through the rubble. The cardboard box filled with bobbing puppy heads was clearly visible not six feet beyond them.

Jed's shoulders sagged in defeat. "Rats! There they are in plain view, and still out of reach! I'm afraid to pull out anything else. The whole mess might collapse, and we'd be right back where we started. I guess we'd better shove Sadie back in there with some food and water and wait till we have some help to clear away the rest of this."

"Maybe not," Erica said impulsively, not willing to give up on all their hard work. "The opening's narrow, but I think I can squeeze through."

"I can't let you crawl in there. It's too risky."

"So? What's one more risk on a day that's been crammed with them? If the tornado didn't kill me, maybe the house won't fall in on me either. This must be my lucky day. Surely the luck will hold fifteen minutes longer while I fish out those pups."

"The logic of your argument escapes me."

"What? You expect sound logic after what I've been through? I'm running on adrenaline and gut reaction here. Now, out of the way."

Jed looked uncertain, but Erica fixed him with a stubborn stare. Finally, muttering something about obsessed, goal-oriented career women, he took Sadie from her and moved aside. Erica saw past his words to the relief mirrored in his eyes. She knew he was secretly pleased with her offer.

She plopped forward on her stomach, and by keeping her elbows close to her sides, managed to squirm through. As soon as her shoulders and arms were clear, she was able to reach out and snag the box of puppies.

The box was too big to drag in after her as she wriggled backward. So she tipped it toward her, spilling the puppies into the circle of her arms. They immediately began to bounce about, licking her face with hyperactive exuberance. It tickled like crazy, and she was giggling uncontrollably by the time she escaped the tunnel.

Thankfully, Jed was waiting to rescue her. He grabbed her pint-sized assailants and set them out in the yard with Sadie before helping her to her feet. "Hey, you were great," he praised.

"Yeah, sure I was." She scrubbed at her face with a damp tissue she'd found in her pocket. "I'll bet I look a mess after crawling through all that dust and crumbling plaster."

He bent and kissed her on the nose. "Well, you're the most beautiful mess I've ever seen. I never thought I'd say this to a pampered big-city woman, but you've got guts."

Pampered big-city woman, indeed! Erica thought. If only he knew the hardships she'd endured and survived. Maybe someday she'd tell him, and he'd have to eat those words. Slowly her merriment faded as she realized they would never have a "someday."

Abruptly she turned and led the way out into the yard.

The puppies were gamboling clumsily around Sadie as if thankful for their rescue. Jed grinned down at them and pretended dismay. "Now that we've gotten them out, what are we going to do with them?"

Erica reached for a cabinet drawer they'd wrenched from the wreckage. "We'll put the pups in this. Then you can carry them and I'll carry Sadie over to Hana's."

"Hana won't want us bringing five dogs in on her. She was one of the people who wanted nothing to do with Sadie when she was first dumped here."

"Hana probably just didn't want the long-term respon-

Decision of the Heart

sibility of a dog—or dogs—since Sadie was pregnant. She won't mind them overnight, or even for a few days, for that matter."

"And after a few days, what?" Jed's dismay as he stared at his house was genuine now.

Erica tried to sound optimistic. "It doesn't appear all that bad. A good crew of carpenters could surely have it back in shape in no time."

"Yeah, if I had the money to hire them. As it is, I pretty much bankrupted myself trying to drag the *Gazette* into the twentieth century. Everything I own is mortgaged to the hilt."

Erica didn't know what to say. She could only pat his arm in sympathy.

Just then a fancy red pickup pulled into the driveway. Erica recognized the man who got out as Zach Ramsey, the builder with whom Jed had had words earlier at the debate. She couldn't imagine why he'd come. He was surely the last person Jed would want to see at a time like this.

"Howdy, Jed," he called. "That tornado sure did a number on your house."

"It sure did." Jed didn't appear at all upset by Ramsey's arrival.

"If you'd like, I can have a crew over here tomorrow to begin putting the pieces back together," Ramsey offered without preamble.

"I'd like nothing more." Jed smiled ruefully. "It's just that—"

"I know you ain't got the money to pay me now," Ramsey interrupted. "I heard you had to go into hock to save the newspaper. But I know you're good for it. You can pay me when you get on your feet."

Jed hesitated for a moment, and Erica envisioned an inner struggle with his pride. Finally he offered his hand. "It's a generous offer, Zach. Thanks."

Ramsey clasped Jed's hand firmly. "You and me have had our differences, but folks should put things like that aside in times of need. That's what the Good Book teaches, anyway, and I'm a God-fearing man. Time'll come when you can return the favor—if not to me, then to some other soul."

"Well, I'll sure be on the lookout for such a time," Jed agreed. "And I'll work out a payment schedule with you as soon as things settle down a bit."

"Sounds good to me. We'll get started first thing in the morning."

Erica stood beside Jed as Ramsey climbed back into his truck and drove away. She didn't quite know what Jed's reaction would be now that the man was gone. She would've had mixed emotions had she been in his position. It was refreshing, of course, to see one human being coming to the aid of another. But she would've considered it humiliating to be in debt to an adversary.

Jed, however, didn't seem to be having that problem. He was in high spirits as they collected the dogs and set off for the boardinghouse. His willingness to forgive and forget somehow irritated her. The rational part of her brain urged her to drop the matter. But the irrational part, fueled by fatigue and emotional stress, drove her to seek an explanation.

"How do you suppose Ramsey heard about your house being damaged?" she began with what little subtlety she could muster under the circumstances.

Jed shrugged. "I imagine it's common knowledge by now. Word of things like that just gets around."

And around, and around, Erica brooded. "Didn't it bother you even a little to accept his offer?"

Jed smiled. "Yeah, a little. But after I thought a moment, it occurred to me that he didn't have to come over. He could've waited for me to come crawling to him. After all, he *is* the only building contractor in town. To reject his offer would've been petty—not to mention stupid."

"You could've hired a contractor from out of town."

"With no money? Fat chance."

"That's another thing. He seemed to know an awful lot about your finances."

Jed chuckled. "Yeah, he did, didn't he? That rather surprised me, too. Then I remembered his brother-in-law is the loan officer at the bank where I financed the new equipment. I guess it's only natural that they'd discuss money matters in the community."

Erica started to raise the issue of ethics and customer confidentiality to which a bank officer should adhere, even with his brother-in-law. But then she remembered she was in a small town. What else would she expect? Small-town people played by their own rules.

Awkwardly, Jed shifted the box of puppies to one arm and reached out to hug her to his side. "Hey, don't worry about it," he chided. "I know we operate differently here than you do in the big city. But in some ways, that helps. If Zach hadn't known about my financial condition, he might not have been so cooperative. I can live with a small violation of privacy if it means getting my roof fixed."

Erica knew Jed was right. This was one instance when the small-town propensity for gossip had proven beneficial.

And if it didn't bother him, it shouldn't bother her. It was quite simply none of her business.

Especially since she was leaving in a couple of days. On the pretense of getting a better grip on Sadie, she shrugged out of his embrace.

Hana was apparently watching for them. She met them on the steps of the boardinghouse. "Land sakes! You got all the little critters out, did ya?"

"Yep," Jed replied. "Does your hospitality extend to four-footed boarders?"

"Well, in this case it does." Hana scooped Sadie out of Erica's arms. "I'll back my car out and turn 'em loose in the garage. It's got a dirt floor, and they can't hurt a thing out there."

"I need a room, too," Jed continued, "if you aren't all booked up."

"I've got plenty of rooms still." Hana winked at Erica. "Don't you worry, Jed. We'll find a special place for you. Right, Erica?"

Erica knew Hana expected some clever response, but her mind was simply too tired to come up with one.

Jed glanced at his watch, then flashed a beguiling smile. "I hate to ask this, but would you ladies be willing to get the dogs settled while I check on things at the newspaper one final time?"

Erica managed a weary grin of understanding and reached out to take the box of puppies from him. "Now I know the meaning of being left holding the bag," she muttered as he loped away distractedly through the gathering dusk.

Hana cackled appreciatively and led the way to the garage.

Ten minutes later, with Sadie and family safely situated,

Erica climbed the stairs to her room. All she wanted was a hot bath and a good night's sleep. She poured half a bottle of lilac-scented bath oil into the tub and ran it to the brim with steaming-hot water. She sank into the heavenly concoction with a contented sigh and let the soothing warmth work its wonders.

She floated in a drowsy half sleep for close to an hour before the water cooled, and it became unpleasant to linger any longer. Besides, she was hungry—famished, really. And her stomach's demands stirred her to action.

Reluctantly, she rose, reached for the oversized towel, and stepped out of the tub. She blotted herself dry and wrapped the towel around her before bending to pull the plug. As she straightened, she heard the unmistakable sound of a door opening behind her.

She whirled to see Jed framed in the doorway to the adjoining bedroom.

Chapter Ten

Erica hugged the towel closer to her as Jed leaned languorously against the door frame, a playful twinkle in his eyes.

"Well, well, well! What a pleasant surprise. My guardian angel knew just what to send me."

"Get out of here this instant!" Erica fumed.

The twinkle faded into a tired smile. "Relax. I'm too worn out to bother you. But I can certainly look...."

"I'd rather you didn't."

"Then why did you leave the door unlocked?"

"It wasn't intentional, believe me. I-I've gotten careless, that's all. No one's been in that room since I checked in. Besides, it would've been just common courtesy for you to knock before barging in like you did!"

"Sorry. I guess I've gotten a little careless myself."

Erica felt at once pleased that he so obviously liked what he saw and disgusted that he was playing this out in such a typically male manner. She lifted her chin defiantly. "Somehow I never thought of you as a voyeur."

A spark of anger flared into his eyes. "Watch it—or I might decide to do more than just look."

She took an involuntary step backwards. "You wouldn't dare!"

The electricity crackled between them for a long moment,

Decision of the Heart

but gradually his anger was extinguished by that overriding quality she'd come to recognize as a basic, innate decency.

He sighed. "No. No, I wouldn't. But you should be grateful for those country-boy morals that were so much a part of my upbringing, because this situation certainly is tempting. A lesser man wouldn't hesitate...."

The desire that turned his voice hoarse pulled at her. He looked so handsome standing there with his shirt unbuttoned, his hair tousled from the rigors of the day. The fact that they'd been through so much together added an additional element to the turmoil in play between them. *A lesser woman wouldn't hesitate either*, she thought.

Then, as much for herself as for him, she said out loud, "But, again, we're not animals—"

"Yeah, yeah, I know," he growled ominously as he turned to leave. "Heaven forbid we should ever let our hearts overrule our heads. Look, will you please put something on and get out of here. I'm entitled to some bathroom privileges, too." He slammed the door behind him with a bang.

Erica was still trembling as she dropped the towel and pulled on her heavy fleece robe. A glance at her reflection in the mirror revealed flushed cheeks that grew even redder when she remembered how poorly she'd behaved. Jed was at fault, sure, but she hadn't made it any easier for him— standing there clad only in a towel.

She belted the robe even tighter and pulled the collar up around her throat before tapping on Jed's bedroom door. "The bathroom's all yours now."

"Okay, thanks," came his muffled reply.

She hesitated. "May I come in?"

"Sure, why not." His voice had lost none of its anger.

When she pushed open the door, she saw him stretched out on the bed, arms folded behind his head. He'd removed his shirt and shoes and was scowling at the ceiling. Hard muscles flexed and tanned flesh glistened as he sat up in an effortless, fluid motion. Never had there been a more perfect male body, she decided on some abstract objective plane of her mind.

"Well, what do you want?" he growled.

She swallowed the lump in her throat. "To apologize. I had no right to call you names. I just wasn't expecting you to appear like that."

"Yeah, I'm sorry, too. I shouldn't have teased you like I did. We're both just stressed out from all that's happened today." He rose and walked toward her. "I hope I'm as refreshed after my bath as you appear to be."

"It'll work wonders," she said breathlessly. "Trust me."

He reached out a hand to gently cup her chin. "You know, it's strange, but I do—trust you, I mean. Facing adversity together does that to people, I've heard—melds them spiritually or something."

"Do you always wax so philosophical when you're weary?" She was finding it hard to concentrate with his thumb inscribing sensual circles on her cheek.

"I don't know," he replied huskily. "This is the first time I've been driven this close to exhaustion."

"Would some food help?" The question was a ploy. Surely discussing such a mundane subject would get her volatile emotions back on an even keel. "I'm going to raid the refrigerator as soon as I'm dressed. I'll be glad to fix you something, too."

"Thanks. You're an angel." He lifted her chin until their eyes met.

The tenderness in his gaze caught her by surprise. She couldn't tear her eyes away, she felt so adored. Then the tenderness smoldered into something more and finally flared into full-fledged desire. Jed pulled her into his arms and lowered his lips to hers. Erica didn't resist. It just felt so good and so right to let him hold her and kiss her.

She twined her arms about his neck, tangling her fingers in the thick curls at the nape. She felt his grip tighten, and she strained into his embrace, pressing her lips more firmly against his. Never had she felt so at one with another person. She never wanted the kiss to end.

But all too soon, it did. Jed broke it off with a ragged sigh, and Erica felt somehow robbed of a divine pleasure. She clung to him, breathless and wanting more. When she raised her eyes to his, there was as much of want and need mirrored there as must be on her own face. She lifted her lips invitingly again, but he thrust her away from him.

"What's wrong?" she asked, feeling confused and rejected.

"This is more than I can handle in my present weakened condition," he said softly. "If we go any further, we'll both be in over our heads."

She laughed shakily. "Don't be silly. We've kissed at other times, and that's where it ended—with a kiss."

"But that was before . . . ."

"Before what?" she prodded irritably.

The cold light of honesty flared into his eyes. "Before I knew what I was missing. You looked so beautiful wrapped in that big towel. I'm only human, Erica, and as easily tempted as any other man."

"Surely you're not saying I intentionally—"

"No, of course not!" he interrupted. "I know you

weren't trying to seduce me. Nor I you. It just happened. But it's still dangerous. We both were pushing too close to the edge. Neither of us is ready . . . *yet.*"

Erica started to protest that this time he was the one overreacting. But then with chilling clarity, she realized he was right. She had been very close to losing control altogether. Embarrassment warred with indignation as the truth sank in.

Jed read her mind again. He laughed and folded her into his arms for a brief, tender hug. "Hey, don't worry about it. We stopped, didn't we? It's no big deal. But it does help me make a point—allowing your heart to rule your head can lead to some exciting new experiences. Let your logical little brain work on that one for a while." He turned her around and gave her a playful shove toward her bedroom. "Now, scoot. Go fix us something to eat while I take a quick shower."

Erica closed the door and stood leaning against it. Jed was right in everything he said—except for one thing. *They* hadn't stopped. *He* had. In his arms she'd become a silly pawn, completely enslaved by her emotions. For the first time in her life, she understood how a person could be totally overcome with passion. Before this, she'd considered herself above such things.

Sounds of Jed's shower drifted out to surround her. His lean, well-muscled image floated unbidden into her mind. What would it be like to be loved by a man so beautiful in body and in spirit?

He'd behaved honorably tonight, even chivalrously, in a land and in a time that had declared chivalry officially dead. His actions just now and all that she'd witnessed of him over the past two weeks testified that he was his own man—

Decision of the Heart 143

not striving at all to become what contemporary society had decreed he should be. He was one of a kind, worthy of a very special woman.

Her heart almost stopped as she realized his behavior toward her indicated he considered her that woman. Her mind settled on something he'd said, "Neither of us is ready . . . *yet.*" It almost sounded as if he expected them to have a future together. Which was ridiculous. . . . Wasn't it?

She'd never before considered their relationship from his perspective. It had been clear from the first that he was attracted to her. He'd even gone so far as to pursue her. For most men that pursuit would have meant nothing beyond a perverse form of recreation. But when a man like Jed Daniels pursued a woman, it meant commitment. Long-term commitment. Even marriage.

Erica shivered at this new thought. Where did that leave her? To this point she'd grudgingly acknowledged the fact that she was falling in love with him. But she'd never considered that these feelings might be mutual—or that they might eventually lead to an offer of marriage.

Marriage was out of the question! Right? Considering an ongoing relationship with Jed meant an ongoing relationship with Willow Springs, and she'd been eagerly anticipating her escape from this miserable place.

Jed's off-key humming reached her above the sounds of running water. Again a picture of his lithe body, wet and glistening, flashed into her mind. She bolted away from the bathroom door, her fists clenched with a resolve that was fast evaporating like the cloud of steam that must be rising from Jed's shower. Her heart and body literally ached for him. And fast on the heels of that longing came the intense desire to disregard those things that loomed as obstacles between them.

Maybe she should keep an open mind about their future—at least for a little while, she mused as she pulled on her clothes. Perhaps she could continue to act as some sort of liaison between Ledbetter Enterprises and the town. B.J. would surely be open to the idea, especially if she pitched it as facilitating a smoother takeover of the lawn mower company.

That would enable her to make frequent visits—and continue to see Jed. Maybe if she got acclimated in gradual doses, life in Willow Springs might eventually seem bearable. Especially if it included being married to a man as handsome, virile, and kind as Jed Daniels.

She gasped. The fact that such a radical thought had entered her head frightened her. Here she was, actually entertaining the idea of living in a small town. Had she gone completely insane?

Considering all she'd been through today, the chances were good that she wasn't thinking clearly. She had to distance herself from such traitorous thoughts—and from the maddeningly desirable man in the next room.

Almost in a panic, she fled down the stairs to the kitchen. Though her hunger had long since disappeared, she hoped that her illogical thought processes might simply be due to lack of nourishment. Perhaps a hearty ham sandwich would bring her to her senses.

"Don't count on it," she muttered as the provocative image of Jed in the shower flashed again into her mind.

As she reached the bottom of the stairs, Allan was emerging from his room. "So now you're talking to yourself, huh?" he teased.

"Yes, I'm afraid so. Being caught out in a tornado does that to one."

A worried frown crossed his face. "You were out in that twister? Amazing! How'd you survive?"

She sighed tiredly. "It's a long, complicated story. One I'd rather not relive right now for a number of reasons." The most prominent one was showering upstairs. "All I want to do is get something to eat."

Allan looked sympathetic and fell into step beside her. "Hey, I understand. You can fill me in later. It may have to wait until we're back in New York City, however. I'm leaving tomorrow."

"So you finished the audit on time. I was afraid you wouldn't be able to, what with the storm and all."

Allan chuckled. "Well, believe it or not, Junior and I worked straight through the tornado. The offices are in the inside center of the plant, and the sounds of the storm didn't even penetrate. All the employees had been given the day off while we completed the equipment inventory, so there wasn't anyone around to warn us. We were just lucky the storm missed the town. If it had hit, we'd be buried in the rubble right now—which, come to think of it, would probably be the least of the complications as far as B.J. was concerned. He'd be more upset that his deal had fallen through."

Erica suspected Allan was right. B.J. wasn't particularly in tune with the human side of his business deals. She hadn't been either until Jed had forced her to consider them. Jed! Why was it always Jed? She pushed angrily through the swinging doors to the kitchen, leaving Allan to fend for himself in dealing with the backswing.

Allan caught the door and dodged through behind her.

"Anyway, we kept the fax lines humming between here and the New York office, and finally B.J.'s people were satisfied. I'm flying back there tomorrow to give them a final briefing. Then B.J. will fly here the next day to sign the contracts. That is, unless Jed has some other sneaky move up his sleeve to spoil the deal at the last minute."

Erica caught herself before she retorted that Jed was upstairs right now with no sleeves on at all. "I don't think he does," she said blandly. "He as much as admitted defeat today. It's all over. The sale will be approved."

Allan perched on a stool at the counter as Erica rummaged in the refrigerator for sandwich makings. "That's how B.J. sees it, too. He's had his people polling the stockholders by phone. He said to tell you you'd done a super job. How does it feel to have won?"

"Truthfully, Allan, at this moment I feel very little of anything."

"Hey, I'm sorry. Here I am rambling on when you're obviously too worn out to listen. I need to get to the reason I waylaid you, don't I?"

Erica grabbed a huge butcher knife from the cutlery drawer and resisted the urge to thrust it at him and demand he do just that. Mustering her self-control, she began sawing ineptly at the ham. "And that reason is . . . ?"

"Well, if you're not too tired, I thought you might want to drive with me to the airport tomorrow so you can keep the car. That way you'll have transportation after I'm gone. Only trouble is, I'm leaving at eight."

"That's no problem. It's early yet. I still have plenty of time to get a good night's sleep. Thanks, Allan."

"Sure." He slid off the stool. "I'll see you in the morning. And I can't wait to hear about your narrow escape from the tornado.''

Erica took another vicious whack at the ham as he left. Talking about the tornado meant talking about Jed. She wasn't sure she could sort out her feelings well enough to do that.

Hana entered the back door then, carrying an empty bowl. She looked askance at Erica's ragged dissection of the ham. "My heavens, child! Let me do that. I should've figured you'd be starved." She dropped the bowl in the sink and quickly washed her hands. "I've been out tending to Jed's dogs."

Erica gladly relinquished her weapon and sank onto the stool Allan had just vacated. "Sorry for mangling your beautiful ham."

"That's okay." Hana looked up slyly at Erica. "You sawed off quite a bit of meat here. How many sandwiches was you gonna fix?"

"Two, at least—maybe three. I don't know how hungry Jed is."

Hana chortled gleefully. "So you two are eating together, huh? Good! There's nothing like a romantic supper to put a man in the right mood. My little plan must be working then."

Erica eyed her suspiciously. "What plan?"

"Why, putting you two in adjoining rooms. I figured you and Jed deserved the opportunity to stop playing these silly games and get on with your affair out in the open—like I'm sure you're used to doing in the big city."

"*Our affair!*" Erica cried. "Hana, let me assure you we're not—"

"Now, honey, you can just quit pretending," Hana interrupted. "Everybody in town knows you're gone on each other. And we all understand how one thing leads to another when two people are in love. We ain't as naive as you city folks think we are. For instance, Bud Landry wasn't fooled one bit about why you two went out to that old farmhouse."

"You talked to Mr. Landry about our visit to the farm? Good grief! A tornado struck this afternoon. Didn't you have better things to discuss?"

Hana winked. "Honey, that tornado just helped spread the story a little faster. Everybody was calling everybody else to see how they fared through the storm, and we got all caught up on our other news at the same time."

"So you—and the whole town, for that matter—pretty much know our every move today," Erica fumed.

"Pretty much, yeah," Hana teased. "Except for what's been going on in your rooms since Jed went up. How about it? Got any racy female-type gossip about that handsome hunk of a man?"

Erica couldn't believe the woman's audacity. She was so shocked and angry she could think of nothing to say.

"Why, honey, you're actually blushing. I would've thought a woman of the world like you would be used to talking about such things. But I understand if you don't want to kiss and tell." Hana put the sandwiches on a tray and added a pitcher of lemonade and two glasses. "That does it. An intimate supper for two. Sure you don't want to share some of the spicy details of the evening so far?"

"Quite sure," Erica replied icily.

"It would remain just between us," Hana prodded.

And the Underwoods, and Bud Landry, and Emma the beautician, and anyone and everyone on Hana's fabled

Decision of the Heart

grapevine, Erica thought as she grabbed up the tray and turned to go.

Hana seemed to be enjoying herself immensely, however. She took one final parting shot. "You know, it wouldn't trouble me none if I had just one bed instead of two to make up tomorrow in your and Jed's rooms."

Erica didn't bother to respond as she fled the kitchen. What was the use? No matter how she and Jed behaved tonight, rumors that they'd slept together would be all over town tomorrow. Nothing had changed in small-town America since her childhood. The gossip mongers never let the facts get in the way of a good story. The lemonade was sloshing dangerously about in the pitcher by the time she reached her room.

The connecting doors stood open, and Jed, once more fully clad, rushed in from his room to help her with the tray. "There's a table by the window in my room where we can eat," he announced, "if you'll bring in another chair."

"By the window, you say?" Erica ranted irritably. "No way! Who knows how many pairs of binoculars are trained through that window right now, watching our every move!" For emphasis, she charged over and closed her blinds.

Jed stared at her in confusion. "Say, what's come over you?"

"I just had a particularly disturbing conversation with Hana. It seems there's a whole network of people in this town keeping track of our activities minute by minute and passing along intimate tidbits—real or imagined—about our relationship. They all but have us in bed together right now, having a torrid affair straight out of the tabloids!"

Jed set the tray on the dresser and reached for her. "Hey, calm down. Surely you're exaggerating."

"Oh, am I?" She shrugged away from him. "Well, you should know that over the last two weeks, Hana has known enough about our whereabouts to indicate she has an information network that easily rivals the CIA!"

Jed smiled benignly. "I still think you're overreacting. Since you're the most glamorous thing to hit this town in years, it's only natural for people to be curious about the things you do—and who you do them with."

"Well, excuse me for being concerned about my reputation—and yours!" she cried. "I suppose you don't mind this blatant invasion of our privacy?"

"Of course I mind. But you're well past minding. You're furious. With Hana, of all people. Why, she's been nothing but kind to you."

"True. But that doesn't entitle her to stick her nose in my business. She's a meddling old busybody—that's all there is to it!"

"Now, wait a minute. That statement is a bit harsh. Hana was probably just joking around. I'm a deacon in my church. She knows I don't routinely have torrid affairs."

"Fine. Look on it as a harmless joke if you want. I don't see it that way. Where I come from, people have better things to do with their lives than gossip and meddle in other people's business."

"Yeah, like concocting grandiose schemes and engineering corporate takeovers. That's only meddling on a grander scale, if you ask me. And it allows you to stick your nose in the business of hundreds of people at one time."

Decision of the Heart

Erica was brought up short by the hard edge of anger in his voice. "Just what do you mean by that crack?"

"I mean, I'm sick and tired of hearing how life in the big city is so far superior to life here in Willow Springs. You take a cheap shot at this town every chance you get, and I'm fed up! No one forced you to come here. You and the other wheeler-dealers at Ledbetter Enterprises dealt yourselves into our lives. And you should at least have the decency to treat our life-style with a little respect. Most people who live here do so by choice, not because they couldn't have something different if they wanted it. They are not second-class citizens, Erica, and you have no right to look down on them."

"Me look down on *them?* Ha! That's a laugh. They're the ones always watching for some reason to criticize and ridicule—like they're doing now with us. What more juicy grist could they find for their rumor mills than to catch us in a compromising situation. And I, for one, think more of my reputation than to allow them to do that!"

Hurt now vied with the anger in Jed's eyes. But, in the end, anger won out. "Well, I'm glad to learn that having your name linked with mine romantically would be such an embarrassment to you."

She gasped. "Oh, Jed, I didn't mean it that way!"

He stared at her for a long moment and gradually the anger faded. But there was nothing left of the earlier adoration she'd seen on his face. His gaze was cold, measuring, analytical—as if he were distancing himself from her for the final time.

She tried again to explain. "It's just this town. It's—"

"—not for you. Yeah, I know. And I think I can guess

the reasons. No deals working here that affect the stock market. No possibility of pulling down a six-figure salary."

"Among other things." He hadn't guessed the main reason for her aversion to the town, but the ones he'd given *had* crossed her mind. She might as well let him think her mercenary and power hungry. To correct him would require getting into areas she'd rather not discuss.

"I thought so." He poured himself a glass of lemonade and picked up his plate from the tray. "I suppose we should call it a night, then. I have a feeling things are going to deteriorate from here." He walked slowly to the door and paused for a moment. "Good-bye, Erica."

A lump rose in her throat. He'd said good-bye—not good night. She tried to keep her voice steady as she answered. "Good-bye, Jed."

She closed the door behind him and stood leaning against it, remembering the euphoria she'd felt earlier when she'd stood in the same spot and listened to him in the shower. The euphoria had been short-lived, she thought bitterly as tears filled her eyes. But, after all, this was happening for the best.

Jed's reaction to Hana's insulting behavior had proven that to Erica. He didn't have a clue about where she was coming from. And he probably never would. They were from two different worlds. His upbringing had given him the self-esteem and security he needed to endure such attacks without feeling threatened. She hadn't been afforded that luxury.

Hana's words, however harmless they were meant, had opened old wounds. She simply didn't have the strength to face down such rumors—no matter how compelling her attraction to Jed. Small-town living wasn't for her, while

Decision of the Heart 153

Jed obviously thrived on it. They could never build a life together. She needed to accept that fact once and for all. Jed apparently had. That's why he'd said good-bye.

Allan took his eyes off the road to glance over at Erica. "My, you're certainly a talkative traveling companion this morning," he teased.

Erica was slouched in the seat next to him pretending to nap. Apparently her efforts to avoid conversation on the drive to Oklahoma City weren't fooling Allan. She sat up reluctantly. "Sorry. I didn't sleep well last night."

His eyes flashed mischievously. "Any particular reason for your insomnia?"

"Too much stimulation yesterday, I guess—the tornado and all."

"And what about the stimulation of last night?"

She glowered darkly. "What are you talking about?"

"Oh, just that Hana intimated this morning that you and Jed might have become more than friends during the course of the evening."

"Did she come right out and say we slept together?" Erica demanded.

"Not in so many words. Let's just say she hinted at it strongly."

"Well, it's a lie! Admittedly, Jed and I are attracted to each other, but that's as far as it goes. Neither of us is the type to settle for a cheap, one-night stand, and there's no way our relationship could develop into anything more. We both saw that and backed off."

"That's too bad," Allan said sadly. "You and Jed just seem right together. I was hoping you'd met the man of your dreams."

Erica shook her head emphatically. "There are too many practical reasons why it wouldn't work out."

"Careful, Erica," Allan warned. "The sort of rightness I mentioned is rare. You should think twice before you throw it away."

"Believe me, I've thought about it a lot more than twice."

He seemed to sense her agitation. He changed the subject. "I called my ex-wife, Peg, one evening last week. We talked for over an hour."

"About anything significant?"

"Maybe. I told her I'd be back in New York this weekend. We made a date to finish our discussion then. She and I once had that rightness between us. Then I got all caught up in climbing the corporate ladder at Ledbetter Enterprises."

Erica didn't miss the note of repressed bitterness in his voice. "Surely you're not thinking of quitting, are you? You have years invested in building your career with the company."

"I'd consider it if Peg wanted me to. I'm going to broach the subject this weekend and see how she reacts. It would be worth it if we can get back together. Surely I can find another position that won't require all this travel—maybe in a nice, quiet town like Willow Springs."

Erica crossed her arms defiantly. "Well, I think you'll be bored out of your skull in a small town. There's literally nothing to do, and you'll have nosy townspeople spying on you and gossiping about your every move."

"So that's what's got you so riled up. You shouldn't let a little gossip bother you, Erica. You just have to confront people like Hana and make them back down. If that happens a few times, they learn to keep their mouths shut."

"It's not worth the effort. It's just easier to live in the city where people have better things to do than sneak around spying on each other."

Allan shrugged. "I guess it depends on your perspective. To me, the benefits of living in a small town seem to outweigh the problems."

"Well, I disagree. And I grew up in a small town."

Allan cocked an eyebrow. "Really? I thought you were big city born and bred. You never spoke of your childhood."

"That's because I don't like to talk about it. Or even think about it. It was that bad. And I'm not exaggerating."

Again Allan didn't force the issue. He reached across and patted her arm. "Sorry," he said, then fell silent.

Erica didn't acknowledge his expression of sympathy. She merely switched the conversation to safer subjects. They spent the remainder of the trip discussing last-minute details concerning the sale.

At the Will Rogers Airport in Oklahoma City, Erica walked with Allan into the terminal. It occurred to her as she tagged along to the departure gate that she was actually clinging to him. It was a first for her. Who would've thought that sassy, independent Erica Stone would ever need the comfort of a friend?

If Allan thought anything of it, he didn't comment. As his flight was announced he bent and kissed her on the cheek. "Well, hang in there for another twenty-four hours and you're home free. Be careful on the drive back to Willow Springs. Strange, isn't it? You can't wait to leave the place, and I'm sad to be going."

"That's the irony of things, I suppose," Erica replied.

"Yeah, I suppose. Try to stick close to Junior today. He's going to be lost without me."

"I know. Keeping him calmed down will probably turn into a major project. In fact, I might settle into that office he gave you at the plant to make my last-minute phone calls. The pay phone at the boardinghouse is not very private." She didn't add that she wanted to avoid any risk of contact with Jed. "Have a good flight."

Erica lifted her hand in a final wave as Allan disappeared down the long walkway to the plane. He was truly a nice guy. She wished him the best. Especially with Peg. It would be heartening to know that sometimes things worked out right for somebody.

It was approaching midnight when Erica returned to the boardinghouse. She was nearly exhausted. She'd pushed herself relentlessly throughout the day. She'd checked with the mayor and City Council, and had called B.J. numerous times to verify his schedule. All seemed in order.

The city leaders, on their own, had reserved the Town Hall for the stockholders' meeting and rented a stretch limousine to bring B.J. and his party from the airport. In typical small-town fashion, various groups were providing the refreshments for an elaborate reception afterwards. The town was going all out to show support for the sale. A sign of her complete victory, Erica thought glumly. She wondered how Jed was feeling right now about that victory. She'd succeeded remarkably well in avoiding him all day. She had a hunch it was because he was working just as hard to avoid her.

When she entered the house, Erica was surprised to find

Hana still up. The landlady appeared quite ill at ease as she asked Erica to join her in the parlor. Erica did so reluctantly.

Hana twisted her hands nervously. "I'll come right to the point. I'm sorry I spoke out of turn last night about you and Jed. Jed waylaid me this morning and told me how upset you was. He made it real clear nothing improper happened between you two. He said you wasn't that kind of girl."

The woman's apology took Erica completely by surprise. She recalled Allan's advice about facing up to Hana. Maybe it really *was* that simple.

"I hope you'll forgive me," Hana said emotionally.

Erica swallowed the lump in her throat. "Yes, of course."

Hana looked relieved. "Good. I know I ought to watch my tongue, but the urge to gossip just overwhelms me sometimes. Jed let me know in no uncertain terms, though, that you and him was just friends. I guess I upset him, too. He picked up his dogs late this afternoon and said he wouldn't be back tonight."

"Oh?" Erica did her best to sound nonchalant. "Where did he go?"

"Back to his house, I reckon. Apparently Zach Ramsey's men got enough done today that the place is livable again."

"I see," Erica said simply. So there would be no problem at all avoiding Jed now. And that was what she wanted, wasn't it? She smiled wanly. "Well, if that's all, I guess I'll go on to bed. It promises to be a long day tomorrow, and I'm very tired."

Chapter Eleven

The feeling of complete exhaustion still clung to Erica the next morning as she moved with the enthusiastic crowd of townspeople out onto the airport runway to welcome B.J. Ledbetter to Willow Springs.

Her night's sleep had been fitful, and she'd awakened feeling dull-witted and depressed. The one thought that kept her going was that soon all this would be over and she could make her escape. She simply had to leave and not look back—for her own sanity. Every fiber of her being cried out for peace. And she couldn't find that peace here.

She stopped beside Mayor Ferris at the bottom of the metal ramp and waited for the plane's passengers to disembark. B.J. himself was first to appear. He paused dramatically in the doorway to wave an expansive greeting.

Erica stood staring up at him with a strange detachment. Perhaps it was her new jaded perspective, but for the first time she noticed a hard predator's gleam in his eyes. He was playing the crowd expertly. He looked particularly distinguished and successful today, his polished air of prosperity in sharp contrast to the slightly shabby Sunday best of the townspeople. She could sense their awe as they crowded in a little closer, perhaps hoping some of his prosperity would rub off on them—as it most certainly would if he followed through on his stated plans for the lawn mower

Decision of the Heart

company. And the people would have her to thank for any future affluence.

Why couldn't she shake the feeling that maybe she hadn't done them such a big favor after all?

Off to the left, a camera strobe flashed. She whirled, expecting to find Jed. She saw Pete instead. Strange that Jed wouldn't cover such an important story himself. But then perhaps the sale was more of a personal defeat than he had let on, and he wanted no part in the festivities.

Or maybe he simply didn't want to run into her. Apparently he'd meant it night before last when he'd said goodbye.

At last B.J. finished his posturing. He moved down the steps, grasped the mayor's hand, then kissed Erica on the cheek. His gesture reassured her somewhat. It was easy to slip back into her role as his enabler and begin making introductions.

Mayor Ferris smiled a profuse welcome. "Glad you could come in person, Mr. Ledbetter. We have a limousine waiting to take you to the stockholders' meeting in style."

B.J. clapped him on the back. "Sounds good, Mayor. And I wouldn't have missed this warm reception for the world. Fine people like you are the backbone of this country." Another wave to the crowd sparked a round of applause.

My, he's certainly putting on a show today, Erica thought cynically. Why, he almost sounded sincere. *Almost*.

As the mayor led the way to the limo, B.J. caught Erica's arm and nodded to the three vice presidents who'd accompanied him. Immediately the men fell into a casual semicircle around them, running interference and making conversation with the excited city officials while Erica and B.J. talked.

"Any last-minute developments I should know about?" B.J. asked.

"No," she assured him. "Nothing's changed since yesterday."

B.J. glanced around. "That hotshot newspaper editor here anywhere? I'd like the chance to gloat a little over our victory."

Erica felt a stab of resentment on Jed's behalf. "I haven't seen him."

"Guess he's lying low. He probably doesn't want to eat crow in public." They were almost to the limousine. "You riding with us?" B.J. asked.

"No," Erica replied, amazed at the relief she felt at having a few moments to recover from his arrogance. "I drove myself over."

"Well, don't be late for the festivities." He squeezed her arm. "This is your triumph more than anyone's."

Then why didn't she feel triumphant? Erica wondered as she made her way to the convertible.

Parking spaces were at a minimum around the Town Hall. So by the time Erica entered the crowded auditorium, the dignitaries were already taking their places onstage. Her eyes searched the crowd for Jed, but he wasn't there. She should've felt only relief. But she didn't. Disappointment surged in upon her as she realized she might well have to leave town without seeing him again.

B.J. motioned her up on the platform, and reluctantly she complied. He draped a fatherly arm around her shoulders. "You've outdone yourself this time, Erica. The townspeople can't say enough good things about you."

Decision of the Heart

"That's because I told them what they wanted to hear," she said sarcastically. "Just like you taught me."

He winked, not the least bothered by her tone. "You learned the lesson well. There'll be a sizable bonus waiting for you when we get back to New York. Which can't be too soon for me. This place is the backside of nowhere. I hope you'll forgive me for marooning you here for two whole weeks."

"Oh, it wasn't that bad." Erica couldn't believe those words had actually spilled from her mouth.

B.J. clapped her on the back. "Always the good sport." He strode away to take his place at center stage as the Mayor gaveled the meeting to order.

Erica hesitated just long enough for the chairs around B.J. to be claimed, then took the last remaining seat at the very edge of the stage. Jed was still nowhere to be seen, so she settled back resignedly as the mayor began his enthusiastic harangue that touted B.J. as the town's economic savior. Then that eerie prickle on the back of Erica's neck signaled Jed's arrival. She looked over her shoulder to see him standing just offstage in the wings. The mere sight of him was enough to set her pulse racing.

He jerked his head in a curt signal for her to follow, then made an exit out the side door to the hallway beyond. She glanced around uneasily. All eyes seemed to be focused on the mayor, so she rose quietly and hurried after Jed.

When she stepped out into the hall, he reached over and shut the door behind her. "Allan just called the newspaper and asked me to find you."

"Allan? What on earth does he want?"

"I don't know, but he said it was urgent. Luckily I stayed

behind to man the fort. Everyone else on my staff is here at this meeting."

"So I noticed. The other businesses closed for today. You could've, too."

"No way. I have a paper to get out. The presses are all set to roll as soon as the vote is official." His eyes were as hypnotic as ever as they bore into hers. "Besides, I was trying to avoid this."

"This what?"

"This awkwardness. You. Me. Standing here. Wishing it could've worked out differently and knowing there's no way—Oh, for Pete's sake! We're just wasting time! Allan wants you to call him right away."

Erica felt a tingle of foreboding as she hurried into the mayor's deserted office across the hallway to use the phone. Allan answered even before the first ring was completed. "Allan, what's all this about?" she demanded.

"Something important has come up," he said tersely. "Have they voted on the sale yet?"

"No, they just started the preliminaries."

"Thank goodness! Then I'm not too late. It's a long story, and I don't have time to explain now. But you've got to stop that vote."

"Well, you'd better take time to explain if you want me to do what you asked!" Erica cried. "I'm not about to risk my job and make a fool of myself in the process without a very good reason."

"Oh, okay," Allan sighed, and Erica could hear the edge of panic in his voice. "A short while ago I went up to the executive offices to turn over some final odds and ends of paperwork for the Lawn Magic file. Everybody up there is whooping it up in what I hope was a *premature* victory

Decision of the Heart 163

celebration. The champagne is flowing freely, and B.J.'s whole staff has had a little too much to drink. They invited me to join in the festivities, since I'd 'been instrumental in putting one over on that hick town.' Needless to say, I was all ears after that. I accepted a glass of champagne and started pumping people for details. You won't believe what I learned.''

"Allan, quit being so theatrical and get on with this," Erica demanded, her apprehension growing by the minute.

"Very well, but you won't like what you hear. It turns out Jed was right to be suspicious of B.J.'s motives. All B.J. is really after is legal title to a patent Junior has applied for in the name of Lawn Magic Mowers. Remember, at one point I said I thought some of Junior's inventions had a lot of potential and he should be asking more for them?''

"Vaguely. What's this particular patent for?"

"A fuel-saving device which would make lawn mower engines more efficient. B.J. has a stooge in the patent office who alerts him to any promising new inventions that come through. Then B.J. either buys the patent outright or finagles around and buys the rights to market and develop it.''

"Yes, I know about his connections at the patent office," Erica conceded. "B.J. enjoys financing young entrepreneurs.''

"You mean *bilking* young entrepreneurs," Allan insisted sarcastically. "This case of hero worship you have for B.J. needs to come to an end. You're too trusting of him. Once I told you that you had an air of honest credibility about you. Well, combine that innate credibility with your misplaced trust in B.J., and you become a dangerous weapon. B.J. sells you, then sends you to sell his victims. They'd see right through him, but in you they correctly see sincerity and right motives. You've been used, Erica. We both have. We need to face that and alert Junior and the townspeople before B.J. comes out the victor in this latest scam."

A cold finger of fear traced a path up Erica's spine as Allan's words hit home. But still some part of her mind couldn't accept what he was saying. "Allan, nothing you've told me so far makes the sale of the company a bad move. So B.J. owns the patent instead of Junior. So what?"

"I'll tell you what." The edge of hysteria was back in Allan's voice. "B.J.'s staff of engineers says that fuel-saving device will work just as well on automobile engines as on lawn mowers. That makes it worth millions, if it's developed properly. Junior and the people of Willow Springs will never see a penny of those millions. As far as the lawn mower company itself, B.J. has already decided to shut it down after a year or two and write if off as a tax loss. Willow Springs will die after that, Erica, just like Jed has been warning all along."

Erica clutched the corner of the desk to steady herself. It hurt to think what a fool she'd been. But she didn't have time to wallow in self-pity right now. "Okay, Allan, you've convinced me. What should I do?"

"Anything you have to, Erica, to stop that sale! Those people trust us. We can't let B.J. do this to them. I'll hang up so you can get back to the meeting. Call me at home later to tell me what happens. I'm cleaning out my desk now. I might as well quit before B.J. fires me. I'm fed up with being a part of his shady dealings anyway. I've been suspicious of his schemes before, but I've just shut my eyes and pretended it was no concern of mine. I couldn't do that this time, though. The people of Willow Springs mean too much to me. Remember, I'm counting on you. Good-bye."

"Allan, wait—" she cried as the line went dead.

"Erica, what is it?" Jed demanded. "You look white as a ghost."

"Allan's discovered B.J. is only buying the lawn mower company to get his hands on one of Junior's inventions. He plans to close the plant after a short period and use it as a tax write-off. Allan wants me to try to stop the sale."

"Oh, we'll stop it all right." Jed's voice took on a deadly intensity. "I'm going out there and reveal that no-good charlatan for what he is. Town savior, indeed! Why, he's nothing but a money-grubbing trickster!" He whirled and stalked toward the door, his back rigid with anger.

Erica breathed a ragged sigh of relief. Jed had taken the matter out of her hands. She'd be spared a confrontation with B.J. after all.

Then suddenly Jed stopped, as if reconsidering his action. Slowly he turned back to face her. "It's not my place to do this. Allan's right. You should be the one to reveal B.J.'s plan to the townspeople."

Erica laughed shakily. "Oh, but you have my blessing. This is a chance for you to say, 'I told you so,' and be a big hero at the same time."

"I don't want to be a hero at your expense."

"At my expense? Good grief!" She stared at him incredulously. "It would be better for both of us if you did this. If I go out there and spoil B.J.'s deal, it will cost me my job. Now, that's expensive!"

Jed glowered at her. "You mean you'd actually consider remaining in Ledbetter's employ after learning about this?"

"No, of course not!" she cried. "But if *you* break the news, I can quietly change jobs later with no interference from B.J. However, if I go up against him openly like this, he'll be out to get me for sure. My career will be over."

Something akin to pain flickered in Jed's eyes. "Yes, you've made it abundantly clear what your career means to you. But, like it or not, you're the only one who can pull this off. Why, I don't even know what all Allan told you. If I go out there, B.J. can just claim I'm trying to cause trouble at the last minute. And plenty of people will believe him. They might even go ahead with the sale in spite of anything I could say. You, on the other hand, have all the details. And, more importantly, you have no reason to lie. It's all up to you now." He strode briskly away down the hall.

Erica ran after him and caught his arm. "Where are you going?" she demanded angrily.

"To my office. I need to rewrite my lead story. Currently the headline reads, *Lawn Magic Mowers Sells to Ledbetter Enterprises.* And all that's about to change, right?"

"You're certainly taking a lot for granted," she fumed petulantly.

His gaze softened a little. "I realize full well the sacrifice you'll be making. It just can't be helped."

"Oh, it can't, huh? Well, what if I refuse to go in there and tell those people what Allan found out?"

Jed regarded her levelly. "You won't. I have complete faith in you. And I know you won't let Allan, or the town, *or me*, down. Granted, this may cost you your job. But if you don't do it, it will cost you your self-respect. Is any job worth that?" He stared deeply into her eyes for a moment, then pushed through the heavy glass door to the street.

Erica glared at his retreating figure. Blast him—he was right! She was the only one who could stop the sale. And

Decision of the Heart 167

she had no choice but to try to do just that. Without further hesitation, she jerked open the stage door and heard Mayor Ferris closing his lengthy address. Taking a deep breath, she rushed on stage. A titter of surprise ran through the audience at her abrupt entrance, causing the mayor to stop in mid-sentence.

He recovered nicely, though. "Well, look who's here, ladies and gentlemen. I think we owe Miss Stone a round of applause for her part in bringing about this proud day in our town's economic development."

The crowd went wild with applause, causing the queasy feeling in Erica's stomach to intensify. They'd probably feel more like lynching her after she made her announcement. Their get-rich-quick dreams were about to be squelched—at least until plans for marketing Junior's invention could be made. And knowing Junior, there was no guarantee that would happen anytime in the near future. But, as Jed said, it simply couldn't be helped.

As the clapping ceased, she took another deep breath and plunged ahead. "I'm sorry to interrupt, Mayor Ferris," she began in a voice that sounded tremulous even to her own ears. "But I need to say a few words."

"Of course, my dear," the mayor exclaimed. "In fact, we would be lax if we didn't hear from you on this auspicious occasion. After all, you're the one mainly responsible for bringing all this about."

Erica winced. She wished he hadn't lain the blame so squarely on her. But he was right. She was mainly responsible—all the more reason to correct the situation before any more damage was done.

She stepped up to the microphone. "Most of you know

Allan Marshall, who was here until yesterday working with me on the sale—"

A smattering of applause for Allan forced her to stop. She could see B.J. was growing impatient. She hurried on before he could make a move to stop her. "Well, Allan is back in New York now at the headquarters of Ledbetter Enterprises, and he just phoned me with some startling information that might well affect the outcome of today's vote."

B.J. leaped to his feet and headed toward her. She quickly grabbed the microphone from its bracket and put the podium between them. B.J. was undaunted. His voice carried clearly throughout the hall even without a microphone. "Ladies and gentlemen, I know you're as anxious as I am to get on with this sale. After all, when it's over you'll all be considerably richer." He glared a warning at Erica. "Perhaps Miss Stone will yield the floor to Mr. Junior Carver so the vote can be taken."

"I can't do that," Erica said quietly into the microphone. "Like I said, I have news these people need to hear before they vote."

The audience had grown grimly silent. They apparently realized her news was not going to add to the frivolity. All eyes shifted from her to B.J. and back again as the standoff continued. This confrontation was taking all the courage she possessed. It seemed somehow blasphemous to go up against B.J. like this. He was her mentor, her benefactor. He'd taught her everything she knew about corporate affairs.

Emotionally, she felt like a traitor. But intellectually, she knew it was he who had betrayed her... then used her to betray the whole town. That knowledge enabled her to stand her ground and return his gaze unflinchingly.

Decision of the Heart

B.J. seemed to sense that she wasn't backing down. He smiled his predator smile and turned on the mayor. "I'm a busy man, Mayor, and this has dragged on long enough. I must insist you ask Miss Stone to yield."

Erica glanced at the mayor and could see the indecision in his eyes. B.J. routinely imposed his will on men much more powerful than Frank Ferris. What if the town simply didn't want to hear her news? What if she were up here sacrificing her career for nothing?

At last the mayor cleared his throat and said firmly, "I'm sorry, Mr. Ledbetter. But I think we can spare Miss Stone a few moments."

Erica released her breath in a ragged sigh, then launched into a rapid recounting of what Allan had discovered. Anger and dismay gradually began registering on the faces of the audience. From the corner of her eye, she saw a red-faced B.J. Ledbetter and his entourage leave the stage. Evidently, he felt there was no need to wait for an official vote. She felt a renewed sadness as she realized her promising career was leaving with him.

"Both Allan and I are sorry to have inadvertently been a part of this deception," she concluded. "We were taken in as much as you were. It's difficult for me to say this, after working so hard to convince you otherwise. But I now urge you to vote against selling Lawn Magic Mowers to Ledbetter Enterprises. Lawn Magic was once a profitable enterprise, and now, with this new invention of Mr. Carver's, it has the potential to be again in the future."

Her words failed to erase the worried frowns that had settled on the faces of the townspeople. The expressions were reflections of the hopeless despair she was feeling to some extent on their behalf. They were smart enough to know they were right back where they'd started—with Junior's inadequate leadership dragging the company slowly but surely into financial ruin. If Lawn Magic had effective management, there would be no ceiling on its prospects. But what executive would leave a position with a solvent firm to take on a floundering relic of a company located at "the backside of nowhere," as B.J. had so colorfully put it?

Then a marvelous thought occurred to her. Who, indeed?

"Yes," she hurried on, "Lawn Magic could well become a prosperous corporate giant if you hire someone to handle the business end, thus allowing Mr. Carver to concentrate on his inventions. In fact, you might even consider approaching Allan Marshall about the position. No one would be better suited for the job or more devoted to the company and your town. He more than proved that today. And"—she glanced pointedly at B.J.'s empty chair—"I happen to know that Allan is in need of a job."

The audience was apparently smart enough to see that her proposal would remove Junior from the picture and open the way for progress. Enthusiastic applause broke out as she handed the microphone back to the mayor.

Even before she had left the stage, Junior rushed forward to make motions to call off the sale and offer Allan the job as business manager of the company. Both passed unanimously, making Erica feel a little better about her sacrifice. The vote was a victory for the town, the company, Allan, and in a backhanded way for Erica herself.

But somehow she didn't feel victorious.

Amid the cheers of jubilation, she slipped unnoticed out the stage door into the hallway. There she came face to face with B.J.

Decision of the Heart

He stormed up to her, his handsome features contorted with rage. "I waited around for the pleasure of telling you this in person. You're fired!"

"I figured as much," she replied with a calmness that belied the tumult of emotions churning inside her.

"Furthermore, I want you and Allan to know that I intend to have the last laugh," he spat. "I'll see that neither of you ever works in big business again." With that he charged out the door... and out of her life.

"And so ends an era," she muttered sadly. With an ever-increasing sense of foreboding, she watched numbly as the limo pulled away from the curb outside. She had no doubts that she'd done the right thing, the only thing she could have done under the circumstances. But it had cost her her long-sought-after dream of becoming a top corporate executive at Ledbetter Enterprises. And it would continue to cost her well into the future if B.J. had anything to say about it.

Although she realized his threats were a trifle overblown, she had no doubts he could easily prevent her from finding another job in New York. But there were other large cities—Chicago, Dallas, Los Angeles. Yes, California might be nice for a change....

A particularly boisterous round of applause drifted out to engulf her. The meeting had once more taken on a festive aura. That was good. She wanted to leave thinking the little community had a viable financial future. And with Allan in charge, that was practically assured.

One by one the faces of the townspeople flashed through her mind. Jed had certainly succeeded in one thing—they were no longer anonymous statistics to her. And despite their numerous faults, she wished them no harm. Somehow it was heartening to think that, in large part thanks to her, they could now get on with their lives unthreatened by the devious schemes of B.J. Ledbetter. And Allan, who had become her friend, would have a good place to live and work, hopefully with his beloved Peg.

Now it was time for her to get on with her life, too. She should just have time to pack and leave town before anyone missed her.

Chapter Twelve

Erica sat at the Will Rogers Airport staring out the wall of windows as the huge jet backed away from the gate and began its snail-like crawl toward the runway. She had hoped to be on it.

She was booked on the late evening flight out to New York, but the airline had taken her name to fly standby if they had a cancellation on an earlier flight. Of course, nothing had opened up so far, and probably wouldn't. Things were clearly not going her way today.

Strange, she marveled as the plane crept away, that something so swift and beautiful in the air could look so ungainly when on the ground. But such was the fate of all creatures when out of their element. She'd felt that way since the moment she'd left New York two weeks ago.

And operating out of her element had cost her everything she'd worked so hard to accumulate over the past ten years. She'd arrived a highly paid mover and shaker. Now she was unemployed. And depending upon how long that unemployment lasted, she stood to lose everything—her savings, her apartment, her beloved antiques.... All were tangible, material things, true, things that perhaps shouldn't have meant so much to her. But they did.

She suddenly realized she had no intangibles—no man to love her, no caring friends or close relationships. She'd guarded very carefully against such ties. And so now she had nothing at all. The utter sadness of it all almost overwhelmed her.

"Hey, beautiful," a distorted male voice whispered flirtatiously from behind her. "Want to go into the lounge for a cup of coffee?"

Oh, great! Now on top of everything, she was being hit on by an airport sleazeball. She swiveled in the hard plastic chair, prepared to give him her most venomous glare. Instead her mouth dropped open in surprise.

"Jed!" she cried. "What on earth are you doing here?"

He dropped nonchalantly into the chair beside her. "I'm just cruising the airport trying to find a good-looking babe to pick up." He winked. "It's a great way to get a date."

Erica laughed in spite of herself. "Yeah, like someone as handsome as you would have to resort to such measures."

He straightened his tie comically. "So, you think I'm handsome, huh?"

"I do. But don't let it go to your head. My judgment hasn't proven all that sound lately."

"You mean just because you were taken in by Ledbetter? Don't beat yourself over the head for that. He's conned wiser people than you."

She deliberately misunderstood. "Meaning I'm stupid, I suppose?" She was afraid to let him get serious. If he offered genuine sympathy, what was left of her composure might well melt away.

"Meaning no such thing. Will you please quit twisting everything I say? I'm trying to pay you a compliment. I was proud of you for having the courage to admit your mistake before the whole town and for telling them how to solve their problems without Ledbetter Enterprises. Your suggestion of hiring Allan was brilliant. He's just what the company—and Junior—needs."

"Thanks." Erica looked away. He'd managed to get serious despite her best efforts.

Jed reached a finger across and gently turned her face back toward him. "Just one question. Why'd you leave before folks had a chance to thank you?"

"There was no real reason to stay. Nothing's changed."

"Don't be silly. Everything's changed. I got back to that meeting before it adjourned today, and I suggested to Junior and the stockholders that they hire you as marketing director. They heartily agreed. They want you to come back and help them figure out how best to sell that wonderful gadget Junior so accidentally invented. When I called Allan in New York to fill him in on all that had happened, he told me the device can be adapted for all internal-combustion engines. That means it could be marketed worldwide. So, conceivably, you could end up flying all over the globe if you accept their offer."

Erica felt her heart jump excitedly at the prospect and potential of such a position. Together, she and Allan could work wonders with that company. Why, the opportunities would be unlimited—

With great effort, she caught herself before her unruly feelings got the better of her good sense. As she'd told Jed only a minute ago, basically nothing had changed. The root problem was still there, solid and unresolvable.

At that moment an airline employee motioned her over to the desk. She was at once relieved and depressed to hear there was an opening on the flight that would be leaving for New York in less than an hour.

She returned to stand woodenly in front of Jed. "They've

had a cancellation on the next flight out. I need to go pick up my boarding pass. I do appreciate your coming after me. I'll keep in touch with you and with Allan."

"You're still leaving?" Jed asked incredulously with an edge of anger in his voice. "Just like that you're going to walk away from a wonderful job opportunity . . . and from me?"

"Jed, please. . . . " Erica felt tears welling into her eyes. "I've told you before, I just couldn't be happy in Willow Springs."

"So you have. Repeatedly. But you've never offered a plausible explanation as to why. The things you've complained about would be considered no more than minor irritations by most people. So I always assumed you were merely looking for excuses not to like the town because there was no way you could pursue a satisfying career from a place like Willow Springs. And on that point I couldn't argue. Consequently, I felt I had no right to ask you to stay, since it meant you'd have to give up such a vital part of your life. But this position at Lawn Magic is custom-made for you. You—we—could have it all. We could be married *and* live in Willow Springs *and* you could still have a challenging career."

He paused and studied her appraisingly. "This has nothing to do with job opportunities, does it? Want to tell me what's really bothering you?"

"Not really."

"Sorry. I can't let you off that easily. You owe me."

And on some level, she recognized that she did. So with a curious detachment, she sank into her seat and told him everything, focusing her gaze somewhere on his collar as she talked.

Decision of the Heart 177

Even to her own ears, her voice sounded dead and emotionless as she droned on about painful experiences that had ripped her heart to shreds. She related all the trauma she'd experienced growing up in a small town. Then she explained how relieved she'd felt when she'd finally escaped to the big city where she was only an anonymous face in the crowd and there was no risk of ever again being the object of such ridicule.

When Erica dared glance up at Jed, she saw his eyes were moist with tears. He'd seen through the robotlike recital to the emotions and raw wounds behind it. As she'd known he would—which was why she hadn't wanted to tell him. His tenderness and understanding might break down the last vestiges of her emotional defenses. And she didn't want that. Couldn't risk it. Even as it was, it would take all her strength to walk away from him—which she clearly had to do. This forced reliving of her nightmarish childhood had only confirmed that for her.

Still, when he opened his arms, she leaned into them. And suddenly someone was crying. Through a haze of wonderment, Erica realized it was she. All the pent-up sorrow of the last twenty years was flowing out of her—and soaking the front of Jed's shirt.

He kissed the top of her head. "It's okay, baby. Go ahead and cry."

Finally she laughed shakily and fished in her purse for a tissue. "Th-thanks," she sniffed. "I don't know what came over me."

He grinned. "I rather enjoyed it, despite feeling a bit soggy."

She dabbed at her eyes. "Will you be serious for once?"

Jed eyes darkened with emotion. "Okay, you want serious? Here goes. I'm so sorry you had to endure all that as a child. I wish I could alter the past and take away your pain. But I can't. The only option at this point is to accept what's happened and make the best of it. And you've already done that to a great extent. There's just one area you're not seeing clearly. It's irrational to blame your hometown—and thus all small towns—for your unhappy childhood."

Erica stiffened and tried to draw away from him, but he held her fast. "Don't get mad. Just listen. Growing up with an alcoholic father was the real cause of your problem. As a little girl, you simply loved your daddy too much to blame him. So you made the town the scapegoat. But if he'd been a responsible parent who'd supported you properly, given you decent clothes and such, the others would've had no reason to gossip and make fun of you."

"Now, just a minute—"

"I know it's hard," he interrupted forcibly, "but you've got to look at this objectively for once. You can't believe you would've had it any easier growing up in the big city under those same circumstances. There you would've been just another face in a swarm of ghetto children whose numbers were so daunting no one child could be singled out as deserving of aid. In fact, you might well have had a much rougher time. Inner-city kids routinely face drugs, street crime, gang violence. So you would've had to deal with an additional element of physical danger as well as the psychological trauma."

Erica had to admit she'd never considered the perspective Jed was forcing upon her now. As she continued to stare into his earnest blue eyes, her hostility gradually melted away. At last she sighed. "You're right, of course. All these years I've thought of my father as a helpless victim.

Decision of the Heart

And I guess in some ways he was. But, like you said, he did have choices. And he *chose* to ignore his responsibility to me in favor of drowning his own sorrow. I guess I haven't wanted to face that before because I didn't want all the pain I suffered to be his fault."

Jed looked relieved. "Well, I'm glad you're still capable of keeping an open mind. And what I said doesn't minimize the guilt of the townspeople. There's no excuse for their being so unkind to you."

"No, there isn't, is there?" she said ruefully. "But, as you pointed out, I probably wouldn't have had it any easier anywhere else. . . . Which merely speaks of the universal cruelty of mankind, I suppose."

Jed winced visibly. "Oh, baby, don't say such things."

"Sorry for sounding so cynical. I guess old thought patterns die hard. At any rate, you've certainly given me some things to think about."

"But I haven't succeeded in changing your mind about leaving?"

She shook her head. "No."

"But why?"

How could she ever explain to him the complicated journey that had led her to the painful conclusion that a marriage between them simply wouldn't work? "You wouldn't understand," she said at last.

"Try me."

She stared at him for a moment. She supposed she had to make the effort. "Everything you've said today makes sense. And eventually I'm sure it will temper my prejudice against small towns. But I still have no desire to live in one and again face the constant gossip and morbid curiosity of thoughtless people. And no matter what you say about the virtues of Willow Springs, we've both been victims there in the past and would continue to be."

He sighed. "You're right. And if it bothers you that much to have people poking their noses into your private business, you could never be happy in Willow Springs."

Erica's last spark of hope died with his words. She hadn't expected him to so readily agree with her. So she'd been right all along. They had no future together. "Then I guess this is good-bye—"

He still refused to release her. "Not so fast."

"Jed, please," she pleaded. "Why drag this out? Let me go."

"You've asked me to do something I simply can't do. There's no way I can just let you walk out of my life. If you can't stay with me in Willow Springs, then I'll go with you to New York . . . or wherever."

"B-but what about your business?" Erica stammered in shock. "You've invested several years of your life in the *Gazette*."

"None of that matters. I'm a good newspaperman. I can find other employment. You'll be starting over in a new job. I can, too. In any city you name."

"You mean you'd leave behind everything you care about?"

"Well, everything except Sadie and the pups. Do you think we can find a high-rise apartment that will let us have five dogs?"

Erica laughed at the comical image. "I think that will depend on how much money we can come up with to bribe the building superintendent."

The tension and sadness inside her were magically melting away. And, somehow, so was much of her resentment toward Willow Springs. In fact, she now felt a strange new concern for its inhabitants. "But if you leave, what will happen to all your employees and the other townspeople who look to you for help and advice?"

"They'll just have to fend for themselves. If it's a choice between fulfilling my duty and losing you, duty will have to fall by the wayside. You're the best thing that's ever happened to me. And I can adjust to living in the big city *with* you a lot easier than I can adjust to living in Willow Springs *without* you."

She felt a stab of guilt. "Still, it's a shame you have to choose."

"Hey, it can't be helped. It's a reality of life that people in small towns make it a point to know one another's business."

Erica eyed him suspiciously. "I sense there a 'but' coming up shortly."

Jed's eyes twinkled mischievously. "You know me all too well, don't you? Okay, here it is. *But* I contend that the people are nosy mostly because they care. And though it's true, and sometimes annoying, that you have few secrets, you're also assured of lots of help when you need it, like Zach Ramsey helped me after the tornado . . . and like your schoolteachers helped you go to college."

He sat looking at her apprehensively, as if he regretted having to make her face this issue in its entirety. And in that instant, she was glad he'd done it. She smiled to break the tension. "You're a persuasive advocate for rural living. You think we should stay in Willow Springs, don't you?"

He did his best to appear unconcerned. "That's strictly up to you."

Her resolve wavered. "I suppose we could try it for a

while and see how it goes. Maybe it wouldn't be so bad if we could restore your grandparents' farmhouse and live out there. That way we might just be able to keep the rumor-mongers at arm's length when we want some privacy.''

Jed was practically beaming now. "Well, with you raking in the big bucks marketing Junior's inventions, we could probably afford to do just that. In fact, I was hoping that house would be the one thing that would finally win you over. Why do you think I dragged you out there?''

"At the time, I really wondered. I thought you'd lost your mind. You'd just suffered a staggering defeat, and it didn't even seem to bother you. You were taking me sightseeing.''

"Oh, losing the debates bothered me plenty. But not as much as the thought of losing you. You see, I fell madly in love with you at first sight. And after that, my goal quite naturally expanded to include not only blocking the sale, but winning you for my wife. And right up until the end, I firmly believed I could do both.''

"Not cocky or anything, were you?'' she teased.

"So, I have one character flaw. I'm perfect in every other way.''

"And modest, too. My, I am getting a prize.''

He sobered again. "All kidding aside, it really shook me up to realize the vote was going against me. For the first time, it dawned on me that I might actually lose you, too. I'd done everything in my power to sell you on the town—*and me*. To no avail. Now, unless something drastic happened, you'd be leaving in two days. Then it occurred to me that if I could get you to visualize what our life together would be like, maybe you'd want to stay. And I almost succeeded, didn't I? Up there in the bedroom at the farmhouse, the old chemistry was kicking in...."

"Oh, you succeeded admirably. Until Bud Landry showed up."

"But even that didn't ruin things completely. I could tell you were beginning to weaken. All I had to do was build on that."

"So that's why you remained so cheerful and accommodating throughout the rest of the day. I couldn't believe you took all that tragedy so well—especially the tornado damage to your house."

"I told you, none of that really mattered to me. How could I be discouraged when I still had a chance to win the real prize—you. You should've seen me after we had that fight at the boardinghouse, however. Man, was I depressed then. These last two days have been the bleakest in my life."

"Yeah, for me, too." Erica felt warm all over as she thought of the patience, effort, and creativity he'd put into wooing her. She was lucky to have him—and even more lucky he hadn't given up on her somewhere along the line, considering all the trouble she'd caused him.

Her eyes misted. "I'm sorry for giving you such a hard time—particularly putting you through the humiliation of losing the debates."

"Don't worry about it," he said softly. "Oh, it would've been nice if I'd been able to rally the town staunchly behind me. But then we might never have known about the potential of Junior's invention. So even that happened for the best."

"It's big of you to take that position when you've been right about everything all down the line. B.J. was up to no good with the buyout.... The sale of the plant would've been disastrous for the town. You're even right about the fact that you're perfect—at least for me. So maybe you're right about Willow Springs, too. Maybe we can build a life together there."

"So, does this mean you want to stay?"

"Oh, I suppose." Erica tried to sound exasperated with herself, but she could tell by Jed's expression that she hadn't quite succeeded. "I realize it doesn't make much sense."

"Unless you're thinking with your heart now instead of your head. Then it makes perfect sense."

"Are you saying this is one of those decisions of the heart you've been ranting about?"

"Yes, as a matter of fact, I am."

"Then you've taught me well, despite my reluctance to learn. I'll give you—and Willow Springs—one last chance."

"In that case...." He looked around as the gate was opened and a throng of deplaning passengers crowded into the waiting room. He rose and pulled her into the midst of them. "Come on."

"What are you doing?" she cried.

"I know how you hate to be the center of attention, and I just have to kiss you properly. In this hubbub, we won't stand out at all."

As his lips descended on hers, Erica laughed in happy abandon and threw her arms around his neck to kiss him back.

All doubts vanished as he folded her tightly into his arms. She'd never felt so safe and protected in all her life. It would all work out. She knew it in her heart—the place where all truly intelligent decisions were made. Just as Jed had been insisting all along.

THE END